A Hobo's Journey toward Glory

G.L. "Red" Farabee

PRESS

ACW PRESS
Phoenix, Arizona 85013

Dedication

This book is dedicated to many godly friends who have already arrived in Glory and are enjoying their rewards for their faithfulness.

To Our Blessed daughter, Mrs. Ivol Lynn Kloote, who has gone on to Glory before us in order to brighten the beautiful streets of heaven.

To Mr. Mike Faris who encouraged me to put these words and valuable lessons into book form to shared with you.

To the faithful and patient secretary, Mrs. Susan McCarty, who was so pleasant and helpful to me. Her Spiritually-Centered life helped the Holy Spirit to flow through the entire manuscript making this a more powerful book.

To my faithful wife, Mrs. Louise Farabee, who has endured me for sixty-three years, trusting and praying to see a light at the end of our tunnel. Yes, she has made these sixty-three years together, these adventures, more sweet and assuring for us both.

And finally to our children, Mrs. Nicaea Overbeek, Mr. Ben Farabee and Mr. David Farabee, who remember many of these events with fun and laughter, not as very serious and profitable lessons and learning experiences. Maybe later?

Contents

1

The Fear of the Lord

This subject of fear is almost forgotten in the '90s. In fact, its use as a deterrent is discouraged for fear of hurting the young children. We have children now that fear nothing, not punishment, death, nor harsh rebuke; not even the threat of removing the TV or computer. Yes, parents and schools, plus the court system, are at a loss trying to figure out something that can curb, or stop, a life of murder, theft, drugs and rebellious living in this generation of lawless and troublesome kids.

Well, I can remember my first lessons in this area. As I grew older, I could realize the total truth of the words—*the fear of the Lord is the beginning of wisdom.* My dad was a great believer in discipline. With five boys loaded with super energy, he knew he had great potential for trouble ahead. He began early, with severe punishment for almost anything and we sure passed the "almost" line—Ha, Ha.

My dad would sometimes postpone punishment and let it double up on us in a severe beating. It was a sad day when one of these judgment days came. On these days, my mother never interfered with the ordeal. She would always be at the old wood stove in the kitchen, I believe, praying for us. My dad would begin his punishment procedure with us all. First he would ask, "Who did it?" but since no one ever knew, we all shared the punishment. It was a serious time for us all, but there was no easy way out. We would run to Mama and beg her to stop him, telling her that he was going to kill all of her children. I could not understand the answer she would give me at that time, but later in life I began to somewhat understand what she meant. She would say, "No, no, he is not going to do that. He loves you too much." Thanks be to God that we all survived those events and grew up to be men our dad was proud of. This caused me to do several studies on the book of Job, in the Bible. I noted that punishment of God's children was crucial and severe. I watch the country of Israel daily, and how the Father of all disciplines His children. They are not freed from their wrong and yet, not one destroyed. He loves them too much. Firm discipline is a must not only for young children, but also for the older child, who needs to be guided through life by discipline.

Some will say, not young innocent babies—no, no. Let me tell you of our first child—a beautiful and brilliant child. When she was approximately three weeks old, we were committed to taking her over to my brother-in-law's house to spend a night there. When the doctor decided my wife was able to ride in a car for almost one mile, we made the trip to Uncle Acie and Aunt Eunice's house.

This first trip was exciting to us. Everyone was gathered around when Nicaea, our wonderful innocent babe opened her big, beautiful eyes. When she looked up at the ceiling at her uncle's home, she saw the difference at once and she began to rebel. She cried. Our wonderful babe would not stop. Every time she looked up she began to cry more. We tried all of the psychology we knew, but nothing would cure that bad, bad act. I realized then that the Bible is true: we are born in sin. I do not know how or when to begin to discipline, but it is better not to wait too long. Sometimes plain love becomes ineffective and a fear must be instilled. If not, everything will get out of hand.

Yes, when all is understood, and reverence and obedience are present, Love is the greatest factor for guidance and trust, but when there is no fear, there is anarchy and rebellion. God loves His own so much, He will not destroy them.

2

JOB 38:1-20

Pressured to Move

When the terrible drought of 1932 troubled these United States, many people had to make changes in their manner of living. This caused people to call to their Lord in desperate prayer. There were signs of repentance in many areas as the Depression brought trouble that seemed unbearable. The terrible summer of hot, dry winds blew the topsoil away. The good fertile land that had produced great supplies of corn, wheat, beans, etc. before, was gone. The cattle in the western states were starving for food, any food, and water. That hot, dry wind never seemed to cease. To go from one building to another was a difficult task. We had to bow low and travel fast with our faces covered from the pelting of the stinging sands. This continued day and night for many weeks.

Most families left their homes and farms , migrating to other areas. Many who traveled away are now living in Michigan. Many others found their way to the southeastern section of the United States. It was a desperate year.

During the weeks that I was riding freight trains in this area, I saw a great many rivers that were completely dried up. There were no water holes or any sign of water to be found in numbers of counties. I hopped off a train in Lapata, Missouri, as the engine required water for steam and power to move ahead to Kansas City with a trainload of starving cattle. A railroad man asked me if I had ridden that train in and when I said, "Yes, I did," he asked me to help the railroad crew to load up a corral of cows and calves. I said that I would. I was stationed near the train with a garden hose and sprinkler. My job was to somewhat settle the dust, so others could drive the cattle into a railroad car and be counted as they entered—50 cows to a train car. We loaded 10 cattle cars and immediately left for the slaughter-house in Kansas City.

I grabbed onto the side of the train as it was leaving, with no time to even get a drink of water from the hose I was holding. I will never forget that dreadful ride. The cows were starving. Their hooves had been worn down to bloody nubs from walking miles and miles in search of some water to drink. The cows would suck on each other's legs, tails, or anything else they could get, trying to bring saliva to their mouths.

When I arrived in Alabama a few days later, I received news of loads of wild horses that had been shipped to a certain horse and mule farm on the mountain. They were to be given to anyone who would promise to give them water and feed.

Within days of being fed and watered, these horses were strong and wild again. This owner had a neat system to sell and break the wild horses. Apparently, the very best and most beautiful horses would sell for $15 or $20. The method of breaking the wild spirit from the horses was to hitch them to a two-horse wagon, one at a time. On the other side of the center of the wagon was a very large, trained mule. The mule would slowly do his duty, following the commands of the driver. I watched this process for many hours, seeing the big mule slowly plodding along, draggin the rebelling horse up the road for a distance. The wild and rebellious horse would fight with all he had, but when this journey ended, approximately two hours later, the horse would return gentle, mild, and peaceable: a new horse with no fight of kicking left in him.

I have thought of this process many times and considered how our Lord has such a method with His people. We rebel, we fight with all our might to have our own way in life, but God puts the pressure on so that we cannot resist and live. Yet, when we complete the process and yield to His will, the good feed, cool water, and comfortable feeling are there waiting for us.

Maybe God had a big part in the drought also. I know many selfish people were made humble by the disturbances of the elements. Yes, God still has control of all He has made. He even directs the winds and withholds the rains.

In Mexico, a wild horse might be tied to a normal Mexican burro. These small, mule-like animals were so used to people and so tame as to be similar to a family dog. When the wild horse and burro were fastened to each other, they would roam out into the desert searching for food. Some days later, they would return to the village very contented, the wild horse not wild anymore. Somehow the wild spirit had been broken by the attachment.

I have often wondered what really took place and what changed the spirit of the rebellious, wild horse. I have always felt that new believers in Jesus Christ should be in relationship with a much stronger partner. This brings confidence, wisdom, and spiritual strength to the new believers.

Today, we get emotional and try to win hundreds to Jesus Christ by way of TV, radio, or some electronic system. This seldom works out as we would like it to. Jesus teaches us to harvest fruit by winning souls one on one. This method can and will be prospered by the Holy Spirit and much fruit will be harvested.

3

REVELATION 3:14 • MATTHEW 6:33

Sawdust and Brush Arbor Days

The small town I was raised in was a typical mining town. The people were very religious and very mean, Ha, Ha. Yes, this work would draw challenging kinds of people. The dangers of the job, digging coal out from under the mountains, caused many accidents. There were many great families living there who were humbled day by day by this type of work. Some of the families would gather at the mouth of these underground mines, rejoicing each day as they saw their loved ones coming out safely. Many, many trusted God for their safety. It was not uncommon to hear people praying for safety and salvation, especially the wives of the miners. Sometimes, loose rocks would fall from above within the mine, and there had been times when these rocks would fall on men, or block their way to freedom. Sometimes gas would form inside the mine, and explosions would occur. Needless to say, this was a dangerous life to live, but some men realized their need for a caring God to call on. Others did not see such a need and became more wicked. This was a place where a preacher could preach the saving grace and the power of God. Men that could hardly read the Bible would carry one in their lunchbox to talk about it with others inside the mine.

Every year, there would be large revival meetings in our area. I remember the brush arbors and sawdust floors, lanterns used for light for the revival meetings, and how these meetings would continue for weeks.

I used to help cut poles, and branches of trees or brush to lay across the poles in a desired fashion. These homemade benches would sometimes seat 500 people. The platforms and chairs were also of the same design. Ushers would stand at each aisle outside, in case someone was smoking too close to the dead leaves. The smokers would then be reminded to move back. Public protection was always present and the event always drew a crowd. Of course this was the purpose, in the hope that as many people as possible could be saved from the wicked life.

I have many, many good memories of these times and have no problem understanding how this fit into God's total plan. Many were saved, which made the town a safe and compassionate place to live, for when lives are changed, the need for locks and bad dogs are reduced.

I am so grateful that I had the opportunities to see, witness, and rejoice in the open truths of the scriptures under in these conditions.

There were mourner's benches for people to use to sit on and pray. Perhaps a concerned loved one would sit near him to pray and read God's Word to the troubled sinner or friend. When someone was saved, how happy everyone was, shouting and crying with joy. And they were always compelled to go tell some of their loved ones, even though it might be midnight. God did great things in this humbled city.

4

An Angel
from the Lord

I was, again, riding a freight train from the West and found myself in Marceline, Missouri, a small rural town. I knew the train would be there for one hour to switch cars and get coal and water loaded.

I began to crawl out from between the freight cars, planning to unload and jump off before I hung on too long and the special agents would pick me up for jail time for trespassing. I had been traveling in Iowa, Kansas and places where I had been very miserable. There had been a hold-up and robbery in Kansas City. The time up in Iowa had been cold nights, and my meals were getting farther and farther apart. The special agents who guarded the trains were becoming more numerous and meaner to hobos. Life had not favored me for several weeks.

As I jumped from the traveling train, I met a middle-aged woman, who asked me if I would spare time for her to talk to me. I said, "Sure, I have nothing but time, but we must get off the railroad property or I will be talking to the police. I suggested walking up to a small park. Just at the top of a long flight of steps, we saw a park bench and sat there. This woman suggested to me that if I had a home, I should go there and stay. She told me she had two sons, one of whom was killed coming home from the West. She watched him get ground up by the same train as her home was only a few yards from the railroad tracks. She could see all the trains going and coming into this town of Marceline. She had vowed to Jesus Christ, her Lord and Savior, to talk to all the people she could about their spiritual life, and to ask them to be careful on the trains if they must ride them. She gave me a spiritual tract to keep and read. She was so honestly concerned for me and my salvation and she told me of why Jesus came to die, and that all of us could have a good life. Our abundant life in Him, but we must believe and accept this fact. She looked me straight in the eyes, full of tears, and told me, "God is looking for you young boys." She cried when she told me of her son who never made it to 17 years of age. She prayed for me, and this Alabama kid was saved approximately four days later in Montgomery, Alabama. Four miserable days changed my life. I was compelled to accept and follow Christ. Yes, I was called from under a freight train.

Why had I ridden so many miles, suffered many hardships and finally met this dear soul in the railroad yard? I had heard this same message many times, but I was not totally impressed until this dear angel spoke to me of how lost I was, and where my life would end without Christ. I pray that she might know she used her time wisely. God blessed her efforts. Thanks be to God for His angel sent for me, and for the Spirit of the Lord convincing me to become one of His.

DANIEL 6:22 • MATTHEW 13:41

Angels—Kansas City

Many words have been used to describe angels, and their appearance, to people. Let me tell you of some events in which I stand boldly to relate of "an angel from the Lord" that without any doubt from me, saved my physical life.

I was in Kansas City in 1932, a very strange city to me. I had no friends there nor any knowledge of the city's general layout. I came in from St. Louis on the Frisco Rail Lines that evening, a sixteen-year-old boy traveling alone. As I had in the past under similar conditions, I walked outside the city until dark, then quietly located a place to sleep for the night. Most of the time this was a cemetery, a quiet place where I felt assured of not being harmed through the night. This had proved to be a good place for me.

I began walking down a street to the skirts of the city. I had walked approximately two miles when, as nightfall neared, I noticed that small shotgun houses lined the street. I heard much loud and wild talking. I could tell the people were drinking heavily as they moved around their talk grew louder. I knew I was in a black neighborhood, though I prayed not to be, but I kept walking directly in the center of the road.

Glancing to my left, I saw a large black man jump off the porch of one of the house and begin walking very fast toward me. I kept my same gait until he came face to face with me. The man asked me if I knew where I was going. I told him clearly and plainly that I did not know where I was going and to please tell me. He said there was a big river just down there and I would never reach my goal if I kept going that way. This big, black angel told me that if he was me, he would turn around now and return back to the bright lights and I would be much safer. Yes, I have prayed many times for that man and thanked God for placing him before me with the inspirational message he gave me. I believe our Lord helps in many ways to persevere and teach his own.

ACTS 15:26 • HAGGAI 1:6

#1 Lesson
on Gambling

A few days ago, I heard a man say, "I consider myself a very educated and sensible man. I am well informed on most things and I don't understand how I got caught up in this. I thought things were going well for me, and now this has happened." The stock market had taken a sharp dive and he felt he was losing money. Millions of people have this very strong desire to get much for little, why is this? I have had good friends who felt themselves to be good gamblers, but they are always losing. Their answer to the problem was always the same, "Next time I will do well, I just feel it."

I was working on a construction job in Gretna, Louisiana, for John Manville Ceiling and Tile Corporation. The employees there made good paychecks, but worked very hard in dangerous jobs. Every Friday night after receiving their paychecks, many would go straight to the Billionaire Club. This was a large gambling business, and what a business it was. I visited this place once with them, and yes, I was impressed. I was not a customer at all because I had learned my lesson on gambling at the age of fifteen. It had been a bad experience for me. I shall never forget that when we entered this club, everyone was given a bus ticket.

I thought, how great that was of them. This ticket would take you to any place in the city for that day or for a certain time. On the second thought, I could understand that when you lost your money gambling, you were not going to hang around there crying and complaining to them. So I could soon see that you should expect to lose.

It was astonishing to see some of the happenings inside and what seemingly sane people would do to change their luck. I shall never forget two older women, approximately 55-60 years of age, running after a young, colored boy. This boy was about six or seven years old and he could run. The women were trying to use all kinds of tricks and methods to catch him because they wanted to rub their money in his hair just to change their luck. How heathen we can be sometimes.

I was indoctrinated against this method of making money on a large ranch, or farm, in Sand Mountain, Alabama. That summer I had agreed to work on the ranch for three months. I was to watch, feed, and care for the mules and horses when they were not working in the fields. I helped make the garden, etc. My pay was to be one pair of overalls and a shirt per month plus ten dollars. I did well there for the three months. The old man Kerr paid me off with $30, shook my hand, and wished me a good year in school before he went on his way. A son-in-law, Otis, was to get me to the bus station seven miles away, but the rains came and we decided not to go that day. So we waited and planned to go the next day. Otis suggested that I use my spare time to play some poker. I thought, yes, maybe I could increase that thirty dollars to forty or even fifty. I had known Otis for the past three months and we were good friends. He had helped me many times before.

The lessons he gave me on playing poker proved fatal to me. He won my $30 from me and I was left without a cent for three hard months of work. The next day, Otis hitched up the buggy with horses to take me to the bus station for my trip home. My summer wages were gone and I felt empty when I thought of returning. I was almost in tears as I put the suitcase of clothes in the buggy. I thought of the events that had happened that year—the runaway mule that almost killed me, the storm that almost got us all, and how I now had no reward for anything.

Otis told me that he liked me. We had a good summer together, he said, and if I would promise to him never to gamble with anyone again, he would give me back the thirty dollars. I was trying to be a fifteen-year-old man, so I replied, "No Otis, as far as I know you won the money fair and I was the sucker." He said yes, but that I would try for the rest of my life to get that money back and that I would never be able to do it. I was not a gambler. I thought many thoughts and in a few minutes, I said, "Otis, I promise." He gave me the money and I thanked him. The promise was a firm handshake and I prayed I would be true to my word. I have never broken the promise I made to Otis. He was a great teacher to me.

JOB 8:8 • ISAIAH 64:4

Unusual Preparation

My crazy desires and my love for adventure have led me to many places and people that I would never have seen or met otherwise and I did not know why until now. I rode in the back of a cattle truck all night with a young sixteen-year-old boy, named Curtis. He seemed to be a nice young man who impressed me as needing a traveling companion. He had told me his home was north of Ames, Iowa and this was new country to me, so I desired to see. it We arrived there approximately two days later still riding the back of cattle trucks.

When we arrived at his home, it was exactly as he had told me. His dad was dead and his older sister spent much of her time helping care for an older, blind man. Curtis' mother tried to hold the home together for the four, including a younger brother who was willing to work at anything. While I was there, we made brooms. They were very crude, but very strong and usable. There was no money to be located at any method, so we made a jig-like machine to put the corn tassels in, stringing them together with strong cords and twister. We shaved off the ends and inserted a nice stick for a handle. The brooms were all well bound together and looked fairly good. They would be used to trade for items of greater value. People would not favor the unfortunate in those Depression days, so we made brooms and butcher knives to sell, or trade, to anyone for anything. We would also make special knives for restaurants—large and strong and well-shaped. These also looked well and were made with good material. We would gather saw blades from cross-cut saws and hand saws, chisel them out roughly, grind them down and shape them into beautiful, appealing knives. We had a hand grinder, bolted on boards, for one to turn and the other to do the master job. We had this arranged so that it could go with us into Des Moines whenever the cold rains would stop. From all this, we got Curtis' mom and family enough money and food to last for several more days. We planned to get to Des Moines to see Curtis' uncle who lived there.

For this week, I was advising Curtis on how to be a good hobo: when, where and how to catch trains, when to catch (or attempt to catch) a freight train, and always to back away, even if it meant time in jail. I had believed Curtis to be a good student in this hobo class.

We had our luggage arranged so that I, who was larger and stronger, would carry the canvas bag of knife material, grinder, clamps, etc., We planned to nail this assembly together and down in boxcars and make knives as we rode—a very clever idea, except when it came time for a rapid move. Curtis' luggage was just his change of clothes and one for me, not a bad arrangement for him. I felt Curtis was well prepared to make his trip to Des Moines. When the evening for departure came, we had already been to the railroad station to survey the layout and make our plans. The fast train came through from the north just after dark, so we did our catching under a street light. I hung on the front of a boxcar, and it sure jerked me into the side of the car, but I hung firm. I kept looking back for Curtis, but never could see him as we traveled under the street lights. I feared for him as I knew it would be dangerous for him.

After approximately four city blocks of travel, I could still see no sign of Curtis, plus the train was getting faster and day-light was leaving fast. My luggage consisted of hardware, but no clothes. So, my first decision was to unload and in a hurry. I made a leap into the dark, hit a garden fence and broke a post off each way. My only padding was a briar patch. I walked back to check on Curtis and am glad to report he had decided to back away—a little too fast. I was happy for him. We went back to Curtis' house and it took Curtis and his younger brother three days, even with their mother's help, to pick the briars from my sore body. There were briars everywhere, even in my ears and the top of my head.

I knew good things didn't come easy, but was all this necessary? I was so thankful for this outcome and we all learned a very important lesson from the episode. We left a very grateful and humble family struggling to survive.

When we arrived in Des Moines by freight a few days later, we laughed. We were all thankful for how everything worked out. I felt that I had been a help while there in northern Iowa, working in the broom and knife manufacturing company. I left Des Moines the next week for a warmer climate. When I think of those times now, I realize the divine Guide and Comforter was by my side training and curing me for some tough work ahead.

PSALMS 91:1 • PROVERBS 30:5

The Wild Ride inside the Tunnel

My dad's life as a coal miner created one of my very worst fears: that a mountain would fall on me and crush the life from my body. I had feared for my dad's safety on many days and nights, with this dreaded thought lingering in my head. I vowed to stay out of those mines. This was the surest and safest way to cope with that fear.

But, Spring found me back on the freight trains traveling across northern Alabama. The rains never seemed to stop. Day after day there was constant rain and this would cause mud slides and rock falls. My attention was drawn to how loose the dirt was and how tons of rock and soil would fall inside those tunnels from the top.

I was riding through one of those dreaded tunnels when no one was traveling with me except my Great Lord and Protector. When I rode inside those loose tunnels, I would take my shirt off, fold it up and place it over my face and nose to breathe through. This would prevent the dangerous coal fumes from the engine smoke taking my life. I was riding outside Attalea, Alabama under the mountain, when a most interesting thing happened to me. The railroad car I was in was approximately four feet high, and I was sitting flat riding in the front corner very close up. When the train was approximately one half a mile inside, I knew the mountain had me buried under it. There was a terrible noise and the train cars rocked and screamed from the overload. This is when my constant Companion was called on and came through again. After a long time of the train struggling and creeping along, I saw daylight again. I looked around inside the railroad car and noticed it was full of loose rock. Dirt was in all three corners, but not the corner I was hunched down in. Yes, I rejoiced, thanking my ever-caring Companion. No, I could never walk away saying I was just a lucky young kid—not a bruise or scratch happened to me, even though death was hanging on my overall suspenders. Thank you again, dear Lord.

PSALMS 29:11 • ROMANS 8:37 • ACTS 19:11 • ACTS 1-8

Arise and Walk

Arise, and take up thy bed and walk." This verse of scripture has continued to stay vital in my mind since 1933. My many weeks of riding the freight trains throughout America had taught me many, many good, useful, and godly lessons to prepare for me a full and abundant life. But an experience in Cleveland, Tennessee during this dry summer is still fixed in my mind 65 years later.

There had been many days when my meals did not come regularly. This compelled me to plan my meals in a more professional and positive manner. I had read in newspapers for weeks ahead that the Church of God was planning a world convention in the city of Cleveland, Tennessee. This convention was to last for two weeks. As a young 17-year-old boy, raised with an average knowledge of the Bible, a thirsting love for people, and a belief in the truth of the scriptures as recorded in the Bible, I knew of the scripture in Mark 2 where the man with palsy was let down through the roof. I had heard great sermons on this topic. I knew it had taken the faith not only of the sick man, but also of the other four to make this event happen. I had never really felt as spiritually strong as these men, but I never doubted the guiding of the Spirit of God within my own life.

I arrived at the large campground outside this typical Tennessee city of approximately 3,000 people. I was impressed by its location, backed against some beautiful mountains. The people there had been praying for this great event for months. Tents, tables, and cooking pits were lined up to provide places for food and rest for thousands. The greatest and most powerful preachers of God's Word were arriving. I arrived on the second day alone, and with a very empty stomach. The tables of food and drink were an answer to my prayers for days.

I noticed immediately people from various places of the world—India, Africa, South America, Spain. I was in awe. Yes, there were many people being carried to and fro by hand, cart or stretcher—by friends, relatives, or loved ones. Some could not speak at all, and some could not be understood when they spoke, but I felt sure God was there because some had the faith to travel for months, spending all the money they could muster, in order to come to America and be healed. Some were lame, some deaf, some could not speak. But I was really saddened to see hundreds there with terrible physical problems, plus more coming. I was amazed at what I was seeing. In all my travels and experiences, I had never witnessed such as this—I felt I would never see and hear such again. Everything I saw and heard had a sweet ring of holiness to it. People were not only pleasant and helpful to each other, but praising God. Yes, this is a far cry from the days and nights I had spent in many hobo jungles, or anywhere else.

As the meetings began, I felt I should enter the large tent where the main speaker and events were taking place. It was very interesting and thrilling to witness. The Word of God came to us so fully and with such purity that all hearts were convicted of our many, many shortcomings and the challenge was too great to bear. A great movement was happening before my eyes. As I look back to that time, trying to explain this to others, I feel as if I am telling them about riding in a flying saucer. No one wants to believe me. As Mark says, there were certain scribes there pondering in their hearts at what they saw.

After each preaching service, there was a healing for the victims. I wanted to be sure and watch this closely so I could hear the names of the people, where they came from and what their problems were. There was shouting, thanking God, and dancing. Others were praising God at the top of their lungs. Those days I shall never forget. Then I wondered as a sharp 17-year-old boy, if this was for real. The cots, chairs, and all kinds of conveyances for these many people were placed several hundred feet away near the hillside and completely out of the way. Some of the people were back in action again and their crutches, etc. were not needed any more.

I have honestly searched the scriptures many, many times, praying for solid truths to be revealed to me. This is mentioned many times in our Bible when others would relate the events of God's healing miracles. Some kept silent, some went to tell others of what they saw and heard. I have told many of these events, but it seems as though they ring true to very few as being works of our Great Lord.

But to me, Red Farabee, I left that place approximately eight days later to get to the railroad yards in Chattanooga twenty miles away, with preachers' words ringing in my ears, and the large piles of beds and crutches proving to me that the faith of righteous men can definitely draw great things from our All Powerful God.

GENESIS 35:1-12

Back to Bethel

Most of my day was used up in a high tower, playing checkers with a railroad detective who was guarding the yards. This sure sounds different, but his job was boring and so he invited me up to play checkers and talk. Since my train going to Kansas City was not due to leave Memphis for several hours, I took the invitation and enjoyed a good afternoon. Then I had to bid this tower spy farewell as I climbed down the tower to catch the Frisco Freight Train. The detective had told me he would have this train slow down just before it crossed the Mississippi River—slow enough that I could get inside an empty boxcar. Well, this all happened smoothly and I climbed inside the car all alone. I found some pieces of cardboard and made myself a bed in the corner of the boxcar.

This was nice, quiet, and a sure, slow route to Kansas City—until I was awakened and jerked out of the boxcar to find all kinds of guns pointing at me. Loud talk and threats were quite a change for me from the treatment I had received in Memphis. I was searched and questioned and I wondered if this section of farmland near Jonesboro, Arkansas would be my final stop. The objective of these policemen, special agents, and railroad crew was to find out who had broken into the car next to the one I was sleeping in. It was a meat car and much had been taken. There was an uproar and I was the only potential suspect around.

I must have given truthful answers and things began to be reasonable. Why and how could I be sleeping so peacefully and yet be guilty of this unlawful act. Soon, they backed me out in the field to hold me until something had been solved. Then, they agreed that I could not have been their train robber and apologetically turned me loose to go. When I was told to go, I did just that—right back into the same bed, in the same boxcar, a lonely and broken kid just dragging himself through this beautiful country.

This experience was not so uncommon. Later I returned to Jonesboro, Arkansas as a Superintendent of Construction. Jonesboro was also a complex for General Electric and I was sent there approximately 30 years after the "drag-out episode" on the freight train. One afternoon, while I was there in Jonesboro, I made a special effort to locate the same place that I had remembered so vividly. I did find it without any doubt. I stood there, looked up to the beautiful heavens and thanked God for how He had protected and guided me to that point. I thought of Jacob and his vision, at Bethel, of heaven, and of how many things had happened in his life, but twenty years later, he went back to Bethel to renew the covenant. Yes, many things and happenings had entered my life between the trips to my Bethel. My, how God guides and blesses.

EPHESIANS 4:22-24

Brand New

As you read through this book, you may think, "what a mixed-up life that man had." As I look back, however, my life seems to have been planned. It all began in 1932, after a very rough and bad year for a kid—Kansas City to Memphis to New Orleans to Mobile. All were scary, mixed-up troublesome days for me. I was running from law officers, railroad special agents, and robbers. All kinds of wicked men chased me through the most severe weather. Hurricanes entered the Gulf Coast in great force. These types of days caused the special agents and policemen to be more on alert for criminals. At this time in Kansas City, Bonnie Parker and Pretty Boy Floyd first began their criminal life, and all law forces were out to run them down. Later, I learned they were traveling the same route as I was.

Traveling from New Orleans to Mobile was the most dangerous and troublesome time of my life. I caught a passenger train in New Orleans and rode the "blind." This is not in the train, but hanging outside between the coaches, tucked into the area where an accordion-type closure was used to connect the coaches together. I had one step on each car for one foot, but no place to hold with my hands was provided for me. So, as the train would go around curves, I would be pressed tight between, or if trains went the other way, I would have to stretch and stretch. If I did not stretch enough, I could fall below to be ground up. So, this was not a comfortable ride to Biloxi, Mississippi, especially in a hard rainstorm at 100 miles an hour. This train was the special to Chicago from New Orleans, but I had felt for sure that I would lose my life in some manner if I stayed in New Orleans.

After this wild ride to Biloxi, I unloaded myself. A policeman saw me get off put me back on the railroad walking toward Mobile in that hard rainstorm of hurricane force. I walked over open railroad ties for a three mile stretch to Ocean Springs on a single track. I knew that at any minute, there could be a train coming and I had no place to climb except down into the water. Thanks be to God, He let me get across the three mile bridge safely. When I arrived in Mobile, there were two men after me, so I ran directly toward the bright light in the terrible storm. I watched them and caught a freight train to Birmingham, Alabama.

This train stopped in Montgomery at 3:00 a.m. and special agents, loaded with rifles, were shooting anything that moved. Water was running, lightning was flashing, and the special agents were shooting. So, that night at 3:00, I cried out to my Lord openly, "Please let me enroll with the group that woman told me about in Missouri." Yes, He heard me, and I knew he had answered my plea. I was truly born again and a new life began. I wanted Him to be the captain of my life forever and He did not have to wait until the storm was over. I crawled out from under the train and began walking up the side of the train without any fear or damage to me.

I caught the front of the train as it was pulling out for Birmingham. By 4:00 or 5:00 A.M., we entered the small mining town of Helena, Alabama. I was the first one on the ground after the storm blew it away—no power, no lights, no ambulance, no doctors. All I could hear and feel was people—yes, people looking and feeling for their loved ones. I cried, feeling so helpless. At day-break, things began to happen. Ambulances had come and I left at the first opportunity, knowing 128 people died there that night.

I went back to school and spoke to the red-headed teacher that had had so much trouble with me. I said, "Mrs. Bell, do you remember that red-headed boy that you had so much trouble with?"

She responded, "Yes, I do."

I said, "Well, he is not here anymore. Things are different now." And they were. We had a great year together. I had sixteen 100s on my report card during my last year in high school. Life proved to be great and I felt assured that all was going to be well for me.

How I managed to go to college is still a mystery to me, even today. I will try to explain how it happened. I hitchhiked to Jacksonville, Alabama to a teacher's college. This school had already been open for two weeks and football practice had already started. The football coach and his wife, Mr. and Mrs. Tom Shotts, were in charge of the boy's dormitory. On this Sunday afternoon, I could not muster up enough words to convince them to let me enter, even for the night. But I sneaked upstairs in the dorm to the third floor and found an empty room with only two beds. I slept there that night. The next evening when I saw the boys preparing for football practice, I fell in line. But the same Tom Shotts saw me and told the man in charge of issuing uniforms to barely let me have any. So, that is what I got—ragged and discarded equipment. My shoes were not mates and were full of tacks on the inside. I prayed, know-ing that God knew of me and He cared. I started practicing on the seventh team far away in the corner of the field, but I had been training in the summer on hoboing and running with no extra food. I was tough and hungry and as dangerous as a hun-gry lion on the field that evening. Within two and a half hours I was running with the number two team and being watched by all. When practice ended, Tom Shotts asked us all to circle the field for three laps and then go to the dressing room for the day.

I was standing near him and asked him if I could run my three laps barefoot. He asked me why, and what was my problem. As I pulled off my right shoe and dumped a big glob of blood that had collected in my shoe, he looked at me and said, "Go in." From that time on, I was highly respected, thanks to a caring God. Yes, this had to be in His plan.

Jacksonville never gave out football scholarships, but during the Depression years when there was no money moving, many students paid their college expenses with vegetables, chickens or whatever else could be used. Many times, different girls would tell me that their dad would be coming in Saturday with turnips or cabbage and ask if I wanted them to put some in for me. I would always say, "Oh yes, please do." Gifts like that paid my expenses through college. I humbly say, I will never live long enough to repay people's goodness to me. As time moved on, I began trying to provide for others like I was might go to college without begging. My precious days of hoboing had made me humble enough, bold enough, and honest enough to survive this section of my life.

As I sit here writing, to my left is a plaque from Jacksonville State University Alumni: a lifetime membership for continuous years of contributions to the college. Yes, this is as God's plan works.

Fifty years later, I returned to the college grounds. I saw my English teacher of olden days, and he showed to me the new and the old of the school. It was a Red Farabee Day. I was totally surprised about who had heard of and remembered me. Dr. Calvert loved to hear about some of my "hobo experiences." We had a great and rewarding day. A few short months later, Dr. Calvert went to be with his Lord.

ISAIAH 41:13 • ISAIAH 42:16

Not Only Me

I was on a freight train going to Chicago from the South. This was during the Depression years and good things didn't come easy, so an experienced hobo did not expect good treatment, in fact, he feared anyone persistent enough to do him good.

I dreaded going into the railroad yards in Chicago, for I knew many special agents would be waiting for me. So, after a sleepless mosquito-bitten night in Chicago Heights, I decided I would walk the rest of the twenty miles into the city. As I started walking down the railroad track, behind me came a train—the engine, several cars and a caboose. This train stopped for me to get on and ride into town, but I backed away off the railroad property and refused the ride. Several men persuaded me to come on board saying they wanted to help me. So this young boy accepted their invitation and rode with the men on into the city.

Along the way, we became close to each other in mind, care and compassion. One of these men gave me a key to his locker and a permit to use his privileges while I was in Chicago. I could shower, wash my clothes, and eat a number of free meals, all because of a compassionate, caring man. I used this for approximately three days and then left town, but not without expressing my thanks and gratitude. I am reminded of Elijah, when he cried out that he was the only one standing for God and God told him to shut up because there were over 10,000 faithful men out there battling for Him. Yes, many good people are out there working for our Lord.

13

Jobs—No

Out of college when work was hard to find, I was standing in a large group of people (approximately 3,000) in the yard of a steel company in Gadsden, Alabama. All were looking and praying for the possibility of being one of seven to be hired that Monday morning. I had no other place to be but this. I was single, with no responsibility except to myself. I was far back in the crowd, hardly noticing what was going on.

The man from the office called to me to come up. I had no application or anyone to recommend me for a job, but he definitely described me and where I was standing. I went in to the employment office on Monday and he asked me if I wanted to go to work. I said yes, but I lived twenty miles away, and if he would hire Eugene Starkey, he had a car and we could both ride together. So, Eugene was hired also that same day. I must say again that God had a big hand in this.

I worked there for five years, I learned much and I was promoted regularly. I was given much responsibility in the machinery and engineering fields.

One day, as the war clouds began to arrive over the U.S.A., I left the steel mills for construction of plants, and installation of machinery, for war preparation. I traveled a lot and felt vital to the cause of protecting not only the shores of the U.S.A., but our families also. I knew then the divine hand guiding me and protecting me through several dangerous and exciting adventures. I was a bold believer to all I met and always faithful to the Lord's house. At the end of each working week I would go to each employee in my gang or department and invite them to come be with me in church on Sunday. Not all replied positively, but the offer was given, a special invitation to be my guest.

Many of these employees, along with members of their families, were truly saved. Many died from accidents in our jobs.

This is unusual, but I never remember asking anyone for a job, even though I have had some good jobs. Again, I can see where my experiences were unusual, exciting and dangerous, but through it all, I could know that I was being prepared for something, somewhere, sometime.

God, through His word, kept me willing to do His will. As we study, pray, and look for His guidance in *all* things, our love for Him grows with our faith. We see His works in all things. We become saturated in God's work. All we say and do will be flavored with the things of Jesus Christ. Yes, this is unusual, but fruitful living.

Learning lessons through all that comes our way, and being willing to put the things of God first in all things of your life, this is where so many fall by the wayside alone. As Jesus Christ told Satan, man does not live by bread alone, but by the words of God.

14

1 CHRONICLES 28:9 • MATTHEW 26:41

Living in the Apex

My best friend in college was a fine young man who was an orphan. He seemed to have always had to struggle for everything he received. In High School, he worked as a janitor to pay his expenses. He had never had any time for sports or much recreation. Everyone loved Odis Clayborn. He was a clean, honest and trustworthy person, preparing to be a director of youth for the county.

Money for my expenses at school was hard to come by. When my bill came, and I could not possibly cope, I would humbly talk to our football coach, hoping he could do something about them. It was known from Dr. Daugette, the founder of the school, down through the faculty, that Odis Clayborn and Red Farabee were allowed, and trusted, to use plywood and extension cords to arrange a place to stay at night and to study in the apex of the large administrative building. This was not to be known by others. We were to keep it unknown by certain methods of keeping lights invisible from outside, etc. Odis was a part-time janitor and had the keys and privileges to use whatever we needed, but not to be too comfortable there. This was great for us. Only *we* were ever allowed to do this and I said many times, "Only God could make this possible." These events helped me to know, time and again, that I was a winner. I was on God's side. When I receive literature from the school and a picture of this building is shown, I point to our old study and bedroom.

When Odis had completed his education for the vocation he so desired, he served only for a few months. In less than a year, he was killed by a group of young boys. I have thought so many times, "Why?" He worked so hard to reach this peak in his life, then God called him home. I never try to understand God's plans. But I do try to believe that in some way, I can do much more than normal to be of value. I feel as if I must push harder for Odis' sake. We cannot do it all. We do not know the whys, but as Christians we must be willing to use our talents where God places us and to let His Spirit lead in our lives.

As I have stated so many times, we are all riding through life atop the apex. It is so easy to slide either way with our lives. We cannot direct our every move and decision within our own selves. We must let our great Leader and Guide control the direction from the apex of life.

GENESIS 2:18 • I CORINTHIANS 2:14

God Sent a Helper

When I settled down into normal work habits in the steel mill, life began to appear different to me. I was living in a boarding house and became lonely. The landlady where I boarded told me of a nearby church where I should go. I ventured over on a Sunday evening and I have never regretted it. I walked up to the church at exactly the right time to see approximately eight to ten of the most beautiful girls I had ever seen. The girls were changing classrooms and I received a glimpse.

During my college years, I never let myself be with girls. I never felt as if I had anything to offer to them: no money, no job, no planned future. So, to be fair to all, I would not be around them, but now I began to feel more secure. I was made aware of what God said to Adam: "It is not good for man to be alone."

There was a beautiful girl who came up to me and invited me into their training union class. I accepted this offer, and this different lifestyle was perfect for me. I had been saved for approximately five years and I had experienced much, but I had no church background or organized teaching and training in God's Word. This I needed and enjoyed. This is where I met my future wife, Louise Bates. She was beautiful, pleasant, clean, and pure—an attractive Christian girl. It seemed as though God had placed me under the large oak tree, and Louise came out to get me.

Due to her very sick Granddad, our courtship was skimpy, but soon after her grandfather's death, we continued the courtship and on June 30, 1937 we were married. There was never any doubt about her not being the girl sent for me. Our life together has been interesting and exciting. Our four children have contributed much to keep us alert and active and God kept guiding step by step. As I survey the past in our lives, I see we were not rebellious. We wanted divine guidance and our desires were not selfish or demanding. Our goals were to maintain a strong Christian home and to enjoy a beautiful life together with our children. We desired to see them grow spiritually into strong Christian children. Our goals were not for much money or large houses, etc. Yet, God has blessed us with all our wants and more. During these many years, I never even remember asking anyone for a job, but I have been provided with many good jobs. God has been more than faithful to us.

I remember when our son, Ben, was in Vietnam at war, he would write home to us so faithfully, regularly, openly, and sincerely. Ben had proven his spiritual life to many good people while he was still in football. But during the tough months in Vietnam, he would give a daily report of marshes, snakes, snipers, bombs—a good picture of a bad war. I remember in one of his letters, he said, God had been so good to him there, and to his young wife at home, and was it selfish for him to continue praying as he was? He had seen so many great things, more than he could expect. Yes, he was faithful and true there where God had placed him. Recognized by all his superiors, he was given an award, in Saigon, as the soldier of the month for some unusual bravery. Even now, we do not know what happened. Blessings flow so surely and gratifyingly when we are trusting and following God. We so-called Christians who have not decided to follow His will, we still cling to our wills, unwilling to step out and so, many blessings pass us by.

It is sixty-one years since the girl came to me under the large oak tree and she is still keeping my clothes ready and clean. She still prepares my every well-balanced meal and keeps a very clean and inviting home, even though she carries a plate and a steel pin in her left hip, from an injury caused by a fall two years ago.

Someone called here a few days ago and asked how Louise was doing. I reported, "Fine—she is out in our garden gathering something for dinner." The garden is approximately 75 yards through some woods. Yes, we have seen many great things happen. To God be the glory and praise.

16

The Wild Ride
into Memphis

We had just finished a good job in Streator, Illinois: an addition for Owens Illinois Glass Company. The spring rains were here for a while and I had my marching orders to report to New Orleans, Louisiana.

While in Streator, I could not find anything to live in with my family, so I bought a trailer. We went to Streator in early December when the weather was minus twenty degrees. I had bought the trailer on the sales lot, but it was frozen to the ground with more snow and freezing happening each day. But, the Farabee family had to live someplace, so we moved into the small trailer. With four children, the trailer was full.

We lived there, on the trailer lot, until the spring thaw. We had to carry all our water and food in and all the waste out. This was a very trying situation, but thanks be to God, He helped us through, as He has done so many times before and afterward and we were strengthened through it all.

I had a large Hudson car to pull the house trailer with. I prepared the hitch and everything else the best I could for the long haul to New Orleans. We planned to go by way of Illinois, Indiana, Kentucky, Tennessee, and Mississippi. We had ridden into Northern Kentucky for a motel room, then continued on the following day. The rains kept coming. Dirty roads and slippery highways were terrible conditions to drive in.

I kept battling the narrow roads, Kentucky hills, and winding muddy roads in storms of hard rains. I prayed to God to help me stay on the road. I stopped in Cairo, Kentucky and noticed a newspaper article on the front page saying, all the truck drivers were trying to get to Memphis before midnight since they were all going on strike. I prayed harder because there were too many narrow roads that I had to pass over and there was not enough room for the large trailer.

Somehow, our dear Lord guided us through all this to Memphis. I stopped to get gas and glanced up at my new trailer where it had leaned over into other traffic. I could see paint markings of red, blue and silver. Some places had no paint at all. Our trailer was leaving our trademarks clearly and plainly. I was so thankful that I still had my family and my trailer.

I often wonder how anyone caught in such a terrible situation, without believing there was a great, all-knowing and all-caring One out there, could stay sane. Yes, I feel the assurance that He is with me in all things, even those miserable, uncertain trips.

17

The Faithful Guardian

We had decided to spend this particular beautiful day in Chicago, at the Lincoln Park Zoo. My family and I loved to observe and study the animals and reptiles, as there was always something new revealed to us. Things were quiet and the animals seemed contented and on their normal routines, but this was to be a very unusual visit.

We were watching the large bears circle one another as they ate. I was leaning on a low rail as my family stood in a small huddle, talking of the bears' natural habitat and how dangerous they could be.

We saw an employee go in with a box of fish or some feed. I noticed he left the outside gate approximately one half inch open, but I was not the only one to notice this. The big, brown bear was sensible enough to notice this also. So, here he came running to the outside world at full speed. When he was outside, he made a sharp left turn toward us, a group of six people on the guard rail. My first thought was for me to be first, then maybe a rescue team would arrive on the scene and save the others, but as so often happens, God intervened.

The bear ran by us, close enough to rub, then ran a few feet farther and snatched a large garbage can. He opened it up and began eating something as we slowly walked away, thanking our great and consistent Guardian. The bear was quietly returned to his living quarters with no harm done, but we learned an everlasting lesson.

18

God's Love and God's Grace

If you had walked up to Brother McBride in the fall of 1924 and asked him about God's love, the answer would have been blunt and disturbing. Ben McBride had just had the motorcycle ride of his life. Since he was 13 years old, Ben had wanted to ride. He had made the big motorcycle hum and throw sand and gravel in the crowd of laughing girls many times before, but today was Harley's time to win. The mixture of gravel and speed left the Harley-Davidson machine laying across the narrow road and on top of Ben's right leg. This doesn't sound so bad, except that Ben was on the opposite side of the road.

This section of hot and dirty Arkansas road was far from any doctor or hospital. 1924 was not a good year for super care and attention to a patient who had just had a leg torn off. No one knew this better than the young man watching his own blood leave his body.

Ben's sisters and God-fearing mother called a prayer meeting that lasted far into the night. Somehow, through someone, Ben received the medical help he needed. Many promises were sent out to a great and all-powerful God, a God that knows and also cares. So many times we forget our promises, but Ben McBride never forgot his made that day in the hot Arkansas sun.

His prayers were for God to spare his life and let him be a true and faithful soldier for Christ every day that he was spared. The ringing of these promises never ceased in Ben's mind. He fought his way to Chicago against great odds, with no money and only one leg, to tell people there about God's love. Sadly, Chicago turned Ben directly around to go to Atlanta, Georgia to enroll in the army, the Salvation Army. Soon, he was enlisted in God's army in Atlanta and the leg was replaced, not by flesh and bone, but by the heart of a hard maple tree. This determined young man was quickly doing tricks on the new leg. He had learned to master it unbelievably well. He had not only noticed a quick recovery from the injury, but there was a Sweet Companion that stayed with him both day and night. If the pains and troubles ever caused him to doubt God's love for him, no one knew it.

The faithfulness of Ben's great God was matched by Ben's faith and loyalty provided to many thousands of people who needed spiritual help plus necessary food, clothing and shelter.

When the terrible drought of 1932 came, which caused the big dust bowl that covered several states, Ben was there pounding the maple leg into the powdered dust and trying to organize food and help for many thousands of people over several months. The great God, so near to Ben, gave him a true and faithful wife while he was in Atlanta. Her name is "Grace." The two could be seen plodding down the streets at any time of day or night. Every week, copies of *The War Cry* were faithfully and prayerfully placed into someone's hand. There seemed to be a continuous need throughout our great nation, and Ben and Grace McBride were always there, organizing and distributing the necessities. It seemed to be divinely guided, always plenty for all.

In the great Texas City explosion and fire in which many were killed, Ben and Grace were on the job before the next daylight.

This same pegleg took many, many steps through the Louisiana floods. Many times Ben would laugh and remark on how he had the most deadly and dangerous moccasin, snakes fooled.

Many times we never notice the regularity of these faithful ones. But God does, for twenty, twenty-five, forty, fifty, sixty years have passed and McBride is still giving out the Salvation Army *War Cry* paper to remind readers that God loves and desires to save them all for a full and abundant life.

The regular Saturday trip today, leads down the main street of Tombstone, Arizona, in and out of each and every business in town. The saloons, dance halls, and grocery stores are regularly visited as Ben quickly, but faithfully, fulfills his promises.

The grace of God still keeps, blesses, and comforts his true soldier, Ben McBride. The thump of the maple leg is not as brisk and regular as it was sixty years ago, but God has complete control of Ben, Grace and the hard maple thump.

19

REVELATION 14:13

I Met Elijah Number Two

The storms had been raging throughout Southern Louisiana for four days and nights. The waters were rising fast! The Pearl River was out of its banks, carrying trees, cattle and barns. Anything in its path was rushed toward the Gulf of Mexico.

I stuck my head out of the small white house that we used as a winter home in that area. It was almost seven o'clock, the time when the four of us men would always meet together to pray and do as the Lord would direct. I turned to my brave wife and asked her if she was afraid to stay there alone while I would be away. Louise said "No," she could lookacross the swamp and see a light at Mary's house. Mary was a widowed lady that lived alone in this low area.

The loud claps of thunder rumbled on and on like a big freight train leaving the country. Lightning never seemed to let up, just a continual flash. I thought to myself: the devil has complete control of the elements tonight.

I met with the other men in a small room of the local church. We discussed how we should use our time for the Lord over the next three or four hours. I must admit that I felt the weakest of the four, spiritually. I even suggested that we not go out that night, but the suggestion never picked up any momentum. I was a young Christian, trying to grow and be true to my Lord and Saviour. So, we all prayed and asked the Lord, "Where to, Lord?" We talked of a man in the hospital who was really sick. We knew of a family that had just had a fire in their home. We discussed a man who we knew was having serious financial problems, and his furniture was being removed because of non-payment. Surely they needed help? We had resolved that wherever and whatever God wanted us to do was definitely our desire.

One of the men mentioned that old Pastor Kent and his wife were alone, far down in the Bogo-Chitto swamps. I had heard of this godly old couple, but had never met them. We decided to go see this faithful warrior in his final battle. Since the talk was that Pastor Kent may not live through the night, it was hard to think of food or something to carry with us. But, after a trip to a fried chicken place, we delivered two orders to the couple.

On the way out of town, driving into the swamps in the old van, the others related a brief history of this man's life. He had been faithful for many years all over this continent, and had made two trips to Europe to preach the good news of Jesus Christ. This Methodist minister never lost himself in theological debate, but rather preached the simple truths of God's Word, which never become old or dull to the listener. How thrilling to hear of this dear one's life! The van knew those roads well and we traveled easily in that direction as we talked about Pastor Kent's life.

We slid in through the back door of a small three-room cottage, far down the riverbank in the low country. From the old logger's road, we could see the light from a small kerosene lamp through the rear window. The rains had not ceased and gushes of water seemed to be telling us, "Get out, get out!"

We knocked on the heavy wooden door and were immediately invited inside to dry off and have a cup of tea. My, how everything changed in this old man's cottage! His wife was a great hostess and truly a faithful and loyal Christian wife, standing by the side of her husband in his last days just as she had done for so many years.

As we talked, it seemed as though I was in a new world. The conversation was of such a sweet, loving, caring and understanding tone. The scriptures seemed to flow into real life to me as never before. Pastor Kent told of the faithfulness of God for his many years, and the blessings that he and Mrs. Kent had enjoyed together, but if it was time to go Home, he was looking forward to it. I could not believe that I was standing there in the midst of this. I thought of myself walking with Enoch. I had completely forgotten about the storms and heavy rains outside. It was a glorious night for all of us. We talked of their needs, or of anything else we could do to make him more comfortable during his last hours as he lay on an old iron bed. Any mention of helping him drew the same resonse: "always cling to the Faith."

When we collected our hats and raincoats to leave, Pastor Kent was asked to pray. I thought this to be somewhat inconsiderate considering his physical condition, but when he asked us to pull him up in his bed and prop him up, I knew I was handling precious property of God.

He began to recite the twenty-third Psalm with a strong voice which vibrated clear throughout the small house. "The Lord is my Shepherd…" Every word was so powerful and real. The valuable nuggets from God that are in those lines had never before been revealed to me. When he said, "I will dwell in the house of my Lord forever," a big smile spread across his face and he bid us farewell. His wife thanked us for our trip to see them and we left by the way of a muddy trail to the back of their property. She shouted to us, "be careful out there, watch your steps. It sure is slippery out there!" I thought, what great advice. Not only because we were on the bank of a raging river at flood time, but because this world we live in is far more dangerous still. Only guidance from on High will keep us going in the right direction.

So much had been crowded into my finite mind that night that many days passed before I could get my feet on the earth again. We knew that the dear man of God could not last in that body. I thought of Enoch, Moses, Elijah and others that God chose to stand close by and see them cross safely to the other side.

What a great privilege for me, a very young and growing Christian, to witness the closing hours of one of God's great ones. To this world, just another Methodist preacher had died, but to God, the heavens were ringing out "Glory, Glory" to greet Pastor Kent.

20

PSALM 66:16 • ACTS 4:20 • 3 JOHN 1:3

True Influence

During my early construction years, I met a man named John Zimmerman. He was listed as a super labor foreman. All his employees loved him and wanted to be like him someday. But we all knew John as this—a good labor foreman, not a good Christian man.

My work was steel fabrication and erection. Consequently, our jobs would seldom be together. Even though our company headquarters was in St. Louis, Missouri, John worked most of his years on Texas jobs.

When we decided to retire from our jobs, it happened that we both selected a small town in Louisiana to settle in. There in Bogalusa, John was known as the most dedicated Christian in the city. His faithfulness never failed. One day and night a week, John could be found on his knees, praying for every patient in the hospital. He was always ready to help anyone with any problem. He was just a super great servant for God.

One day, John and I were talking and I asked him what had happened within his life too turn his life into one that was so dedicated and faithful to God's work. He told me about when he married his wife, a young Christian school teacher in Lubbock,

Texas. She was a Christian then and he was not. During the first week of their marriage, John came home from work tired, angry and disgusted. He told his wife that if old John, the General Superintendent, called for him, she was to tell him her husband was not home. So, John began to take his bath and rest for a minute. When the phone rang, Mrs. Zimmerman answered saying that John was in the tub and would be out in a few minutes. When John asked her about this answer, she stood in front of him and said plainly that she was not going to lie for him or any other man and not to forget it.

On Sunday, she dressed up and when John asked her where she was going, she said, "to church." John asked if she knew where one was, saying he was not going today, he was too tired. So, Mrs. Zimmerman went to church. She did the same the next weekend. But on the third Sunday, John went with her to church and was soon thereafter saved. Things were immediately different.

Now everyone that knew John wanted to live as dedicated a life as he did. What a strong, loving, Christian man with the power to draw God down to these dear souls' bedsides. I count it a special privilege to have known John. He was a great inspiration to my Christian life. Transformed from a dirty labor foreman into a saint, he is now seated in a front seat in Glory. Yes, this option is open to all of us. Sign up now.

21

REVELATION 22:14

Look What I Found

Some people have only one life to live, but let me tell you of a man to whom God gave three lives.

I was working in a small town in Louisiana installing various buildings and machinery for a large paper company. The plant engineer and I were strolling over areas of their property to select a place for more plant expansion.

Two plant employees came running up to tell me that they thought one of my men had fallen into a large evaporator. This tank was approximately fifty feet deep and was used to process wood chips into pulp. I knew at once that I had two men working near the large tank. So, we rushed to the place of tragedy. Smitty and I climbed to the top of the vessel and found only the top section of a forty-foot ladder projecting out of the vessel.

I immediately started to climb down inside the tank to see what had happened. As soon as I entered, a heavy blast of gas enveloped me and I had to hold my breath until I was free from the fumes. The plant engineer began to talk of getting a gas mask from the office or nearby. I knew this would take far too much time and thought maybe I could try again.

I did have two men who were cutting and welding steel, installing steps and walkways to reach the top of those large tanks. They tied a rope around me to pull me out at short notice and I pulled my shirt off and wrapped it around my face to filter my breathing process. I climbed down inside the vessel and found a man still hanging on the bottom round of the long ladder. This I had been prepared for. I tied a rope around his leg before rushing back to the top for fresh air. I will never forget as he was being pulled out upside down, with coins, pocketknife and purse all falling from his pockets, the ringing and thuds of material things never to return.

When we had Lester Magee on the top, but in a warm location, we began to give him artificial respiration treatment. We were at the top where no one could reach us and I had asked Red Mitchell to get the oxygen tank he was using, up to us. This he did and we focused a slow movement of this oxygen into Lester's face to help encourage breathing. At the same time, we were pumping air into his lungs by hand.

The ambulances arrived with nurses and a doctor, but they could not climb to where we were working on Lester. The doctor hollered and screamed to us to let the man down to them, but I felt no—positively not. The body was warm and laying on a warm surface and I prayed for the blood in his body not to become chilled or it would be harder to get it flowing again. We kept this process going for approximately 20 minutes, relieving each other in administering artificial respiration.

When I felt a flutter of blood through his veins, I had to look up to open sky and say, "Thank you, Lord, for a second life for this man with a young family." Some minutes later, the pulse became stronger and our patient began to moan and try to move around. We let him down to the doctor and nurses below by ropes and they took him quickly to the nearby hospital. I did not know Lester well until after this event, but I was privileged to meet his wife and young children soon.

I left the job at once, praising God for several hours at home for what I had witnessed that day. God alone could have guided all those things, step by step. I prayed constantly that Lester would be spared to good health, and become a faithful warrior for Jesus Christ. Well, Lester formed a quartet and traveled all over the United States singing Christian songs and giving testimonies for our Savior. Yes, Lester Magee began a strong third life, not only in this world, but to be continuted in Glory.

That evening at the hospital, the crying and grateful children and mother of the Magee family wanted to thank me. All I could say was, "no, it was not me. Give God all the glory." I reminded the three children to never forget this and to keep praising Him.

Lester died a few years later, but he and his sure testimony blazed a solid, clean trail through this world for Jesus Christ.

I tell many that God is not only willing to help make life abundant, He is also available to His own. We must be found willing to be used.

22

2 CORINTHIANS 4:16-17

Old Corinth

While I was on a trip to the old city of Corinth, Greece, I stumbled into a new adventure that has never left my mind. I was en route through Athens, when my heart was blessed and also saddened.

I climbed up a solid rock hill to stand in exactly the place where the Apostle Paul had stood to invite the leading educators and intellects of his day to discuss the true and living God. These were people who would go to any extent to worship the unknown God. Paul was saddened and left Athens feeling useless and discouraged. Today, you cannot even find a postcard about the famous Mars Hill of the Bible—not when I was there last. We must always remember that our living God is still on His throne. The beautiful ruins of the old Athens are all that remains of its former glory. Nearby, I saw a small church like the building that has a reputation for having been open for over 2,000 years, but no one uses it today.

When I think of Corinth, I always compare it with New Orleans, Louisiana. This was a very large seaport, a very wicked and mixed-up city. Many of the population were temporary citizens of many cultures, as most seaports are.

There was a large acropolis, approximately 2,000 feet high, a step-up mountain overlooking the city. Superstition says it was built to keep out the wickedness. It sure failed to do its duty. Under the shadows was the Skeleton of Corinth—the largest building. The Apollo building housed over 1,000 women performing all kinds of sexual acts in the name of religion. This was a very strongly built building in the center of the city. It was maybe three floors high, 700 feet long, and 50 feet wide.

If you remember, one of Paul's major problems in Corinth was the divisions within the church. Apollos' party, Peter's party, Paul's party, and Christ's party were all preaching their own messages in old Corinth.

I was looking around very closely and noticed a large stone beam that had fallen years ago from across the top of a building. After moving some washed-up dirt from the lower side, I could read part of the Bible verses—2 Corinthians 4:16-17, written both in Greek and English. This is my interpretation as a layman: This is why we should never give up, though our bodies are dying. Our inner strength in the Lord is growing everyday. These troubles and sufferings of ours are, after all, quite small and won't last very long. Yet, this short time of distress will result in God's richest blessings upon us forever and ever. So, we don't look at what can be seen right now—the trouble all around us, but look forward to the joys of heaven, which we have not yet seen.

Only the 16th verse was visible, but I said, this beam fell from atop the First Baptist Church of Corinth.

At one time this city was estimated to contain approximately three million people, but I would estimate only 200 or 300 people live nearby today. There is only one way out of the city and a funeral procession halted out bus as we were leaving Corinth. Apparently, a teenage girl had been killed by some vehicle. She was approximately 16 years old and seemed to have been very popular. It was a beautiful Sunday evening and I felt that most of the population, both young and old, were in attendance at the processional. I counted only sixty-eight people. This is what happens to any ungodly city, ungodly country, or ungodly family, for they cannot survive God's "judgment of sin."

23

PSALM 93:5 • LUKE 23:50-57

Is the Tassel Worth the Hassle? —Yes

The powerhouse at Port Sheldon, Michigan was equipped with the most modern machinery and electronic devices. Even the contents of railroad coal cars were dumped into a large basin to be carried away at full speed. Everything there was set up to dump a ninety-ton car full of coal and to remove it from the pit in three minutes. Every three minutes, a full car was dumped, if all worked as it should.

I was in charge of the job on which this procedure failed. Yes, the complete structure and procedure was ruined. So, we built another complete car dumper onto the side of that building. This was all assembled, riveted, painted and ready to replace the old structure. We removed the entire roof of the old building in order to use two large cranes to handle their units on a certain selected day. All went well for us. A beautiful day was predicted with no high wind. The large crane came in from Detroit and one from Muskegon, Michigan.

I was proud of what was being done and as I often do, I wanted to take pictures of different phases of the operation. I asked for permission from Consumers Power Company to do this, but the answer was no. I inquired as to why I could not do this as I knew the man I was speaking with well. I would say we were good friends and our relationship had been good. He told me how careful they had to be about everything and how determined someone could be to create undue problems. "Why take a chance?" he said, "the tassel could not be worth the hassle." He also pointed to a beer can lying in the grass at the fence. "Someone could pick that out in the picture," he said, "and accuse us of having drinking parties out here." Yes, I could understand his points.

I have nothing material, as important to me as my testimony and my character. My reputation is valuable to me. If we would protect our actions and all that we say as carefully as some of these companies, it would mean much more to others when they hear we are Christians. We could remove many doubts about our behavior, and let our testimony ring loud, firm and clear. Think about this.

24

JOB 4:7 • JOB 11:15 • MATTHEW 5:8

The Power of Innocence

I was taught a very simple, but important, lesson in the Louisiana swamps on a wild hog hunting trip. We had planned this trip into a certain area of the wild Pearl River swamps for several months. There were two very important factors that determined the timing of this hunt. First, was to wait for the receding water to go down far enough for us to get in there. Then, we needed a king dog—"Ole Joe"—a great dog, and a large and sensible catahowla. This kind of dog was scarce and in great demand. A catahowla is a dog crossed between the dogs that DeSoto brought to America in years past and the leading dog that the Indians had here. This dog could be vicious, but sensible and understanding. "Ole Joe" had been ripped open on one side from a wild hog and was healing up. We wanted to take "Ole Joe" and two more bad, tough dogs with us on this hunt.

A few days before this trip into the swamps of snakes and alligators, all guarding their area, I asked the others what they thought I should provide. These two old pros of the swamp said nothing at first. Then, on second thought they said I should bring a pistol in case I have to shoot a hog off one of us, or maybe some animal out to harm us. Then, "Oh, yes," one said, ·

"and get some quick blood stop in case I get ripped by the hog's tusks or teeth." This was so that the victim would not lose very much blood.

In a few days, the water had gone down and Ole Joe's side was healed. All was set to go, so into the fourteen-foot boat, three men and three dogs were on our way. The dogs were keyed up and ready to tear everything apart.

We found the place to cross over to an island area where the hogs were supposed to be. The other two men left the boat and took the dogs ahead looking for wild boars. Meanwhile, I moved the boat over to a good location and tied it up to keep it secure. After approximately twenty minutes, I heard a wild noise of bad, hungry, killing dogs. My first thought was a hope that the hog would not kill our dogs.

I saw two small young wild goats coming through the swamps. They were running, scared to death, and crying like babies as they came toward me at full speed. I knew that goats don't jump into water unless it is absolutely necessary, but they ran toward the water, only changing their course as the dogs came near. The young goats ran over to a large log and lay there crying. Here were three of the meanest dogs in Washington Parish chasing these innocent goats who were laying with locked necks, crying. The dogs came up to these little fellows and just looked, hushed their barking and snarling, then walked away. They were on their way to get their catch, a wild boar.

I could not believe what I saw. I could only believe there was power in innocence. This is something I have thought much about. I have searched my and identified many things that were made easier, and more pleasant, because I was just a young boy. Even several times in the hobo jungles when a fight started, someone stood for my protection saying, "don't touch the kid."

The police have questioned me many times and I always tried to be honest and truthful. Yes, I do feel our God in heaven recognizes and honors truth, honesty and purity. Think this over in the light of the life and death of Jesus Christ.

We captured the goats and brought them home with us, along with the big hog. It was a good day's hunting.

I learned another lesson from this trip. As I carried the wild hog across my shoulder to the boat, I knew that the coat would have to be burned on my arrival home, due to the terrible odor from the pig.

But, my wife never even smelled the coat, and I learned that when pigs eat in the wild, the odors are not bad. Only when they are fed domestic food, do they stink. After keeping the pig in a pen for a year, it really smelled bad. Why? God knows why, I do not.

MATTHEW 16:26 • MARK 8:36

The Paid-Up Member for Salvation

While on a job here in Holland, a certain man working for me lost his father. John came to work the next morning as usual, but when I found out that his dad had died the night before, I went directly to him and asked about it. Yes, he told me, his dad had died, but there was nothing he could do. His sister would handle all the business, etc. I told John to get his tools together and get out for the rest of the week. He could not stay on my job under the circumstances. "Come back on Monday," I said. His father was due more respect than that just for feeding him and directing his life so far.

I later talked to John about his own salvation. He told me that he didn't want to talk about that. He had a man paid to take care of that—same as a barber to keep him groomed, a man to care for his car, and a man that cared for his yard. John died a few years later. He had cut his hand while opening a can of potted meat and blood poisoning soon took his life. The poor, stubborn man had his own way, but lost everything.

Benaiah

On a very beautiful summer afternoon, a very interesting and astonishing event happened that I shall never forget. I live on a five-acre plot which includes a large garden area and an orchard of approximately seventy-five fruit trees of all kinds. Many tall pine trees provide shade for the area and I try to keep the undergrowth cleared out, leaving somewhat of a park area. The summer breeze sings as it goes through the tall pines. The smell of fresh air, flavored from a trip through the fresh pine needles, is an added feature. So, this is a perfect place to sit and meditate on the blessings from God. I was doing this on a Sunday evening as my wife took her routine nap.

I sat talking to a Touty Wren that was rebuking me for sitting too close to his house. I was trying to explain that I meant no harm to her or hers. Many of her friends came to help protest against the intruder, but I was talking to all of them. There were two beautiful orioles there which I had named before. One, I had called Orrie and the other one Oley. They were encouraging the rebellion.

I glanced to my left and here came a young rabbit. It hopped up in my lap and snuggled up against my body. I could not believe what I was witnessing. I thought of a very intense study I had made, comparing the lives of animals and man in God's world. I was interested in the purpose of God in making things and beings and how man's and animals' lives dovetail together. The thought came to enjoy all that God had made, and not to destroy, harm or kill. I felt as if I was living in the Garden of Eden.

This rabbit seemed so comfortable as I talked to him. I told him he could not make a habit of that or he would not live long. "On one side lives a man with a gun," I said, "and he loves to shoot guys like you. On the other side is a man who owns many, many dogs just drooling to sink their teeth into your neck and back." This new friend just snuggled closer to me. After some time I put "Benaiah" down with a bit of good advice for him, "Don't trust everyone." With his new name and advice, he trotted away.

I kept quiet about this for several days, but on the following Tuesday, Louise and I sat in front of our garage talking with our sharecroppers. We were discussing how well our garden was growing and that soon we would be eating our new cantaloupes. I was compelled to tell what had happened the past Sunday evening and about my new rabbit friend. With much courage I told of how comfortable he acted. Yes, all laughed as if the old man had been out in the hot sun too long, but just then, the rabbit came from the back garage door and hopped up in Geneva's lap. We were all shocked, but he soon hopped down and went on his merry way.

The next day I saw Benaiah out in the garden eating some tender cantaloupe buds. He sure loved those good, tender, sweet buds. I thought this was great, except that they were not my cantaloupes. They belonged to Bill, my sharecropper, and I knew he would not appreciate feeding his cantaloupes to a rabbit.

I caught Benaiah and warned him, with a good spanking, to stay out of the garden. However, this proved to be a fruitless punishment. Before sundown, the young cantaloupe-eater was back hard at work. This time, my rebuke came much stronger with a switch across his body. The next morning Benaiah had his breakfast in Bill's cantaloupe and I knew this must stop soon, very soon.

I told my new friend that he would have to leave our area. The following morning I fixed Benaiah a good sack lunch for his trip. This consisted of fresh carrots, cabbage, sliced apples and a few other goodies I knew he would love to eat.

We got into the car together and I drove three miles due north to a nice, similar setting. I got out of the car and surveyed the area. I saw nice homes with children playing nearby; above all I did not hear any dogs barking. So, I spread out a nice dinner for Benaiah and drove off leaving a very happy and contented rabbit.

Two years later, Benaiah came back to see me. I was working in the pines and he came up to me. I sat down and talked to him for some time. We could hear the dogs barking nearby. After a few hours my friend left, never to be seen again.

I wondered what was happening to him—if he had trusted a wrong person, or had lost his desire to flee from the evil dogs or enemies. I knew one thing for sure, that God was in Benaiah's life someway, somehow. This event sure humbled this old man and caused him to try more to understand God and His creation and that they were not designed to fight, bite, kill, or destroy one another. These things could, and should, be sweet blessings from our God in heaven.

On the fall of the following year, as I was strolling through the apple orchard I saw Benaiah lying lifeless under an apple tree. I buried him under my favorite golden delicious apple tree, knowing this was the end of a great and rewarding experience for me and maybe even for Benaiah. Who knows? "God does."

27

Paid in Full

I was at the local city mission a few nights ago, talking to two young men about the direction they were going with their lives. They had told me they were not satisfied with all of the happenings in their lives. One young man told me he was using the needle, plus he had a girl who was four months pregnant and all this was too much to bear. The other boy had just left home the day before. He claimed his dad kicked him out due to some things he had done.

These boys were 19 and 20 years of age, sure regretted their past, and did not know what to do. I told them it appeared they had so many good things going for them if they would get their lives straightened out. I said if they refused, it was like putting themselves in a dumpster to be hauled off to be buried in all their sins, and it could be that their past sins would be paid in full tonight. This was hard, and impossible to comprehend for them. They were confused by how they could go back and straighten out some bad things in their lives in order to get right with our God.

This is a true story which parallels how our heavenly Father pays our bills. A well-known businessman here in Holland owned and operated a good business, a very flourishing grocery store plus a super meat market. He was known for his good meats. Many came from afar to buy meat from Charlie. His honesty and concern for the satisfaction of his customers built a strong relationship with people.

God had blessed Charlie and his business well. He grew from a small, corner meat market to a large, complete, grocery and meat store. It also seemed that as God blessed Charlie, Charlie blessed others. Many elders in need were especially favored. When some young man, or family, were struggling to continue on in a Bible school, this dear saint would help them in some way.

Charlie ran a business with complete control. When he had members of his family working for the store, they received their own paycheck, the same as other employees. When his daughter Joan worked, she was usually a checkout girl and I remember well one event that happened at the checkout counter between Joan and a small, widowed customer.

Charlie always worked in the meat section of the store to meet and fellowship with his many friends as he filled their meat orders. Sometimes, as he felt moved to do so, he would mark on the package "No Charge" and expected the cashier to respect those words.

I was standing in line as Joan picked up a large package of meat on which was written, "No Charge." The small, widow woman looked bewildered as she fumbled in a small cloth bag looking for change to pay. She appeared stunned and seemed to question the "No Charge" sign and what it meant to her. I will never forget what Joan said in a very plain and stately voice: "When my father says there is no charge, he means no charge. Bill paid in full."

I began to understand more of what our heavenly Father says about our past sins, that there is no charge, the bill is paid in full. The bill was paid when Jesus Christ came to take away the sins of the whole world, but we must claim or acknowledge the deal, and we surely will thank Him for His love and compassion.

I tried to explain to the two young men that they were like the poor old lady groping and fumbling to try and pay for the items already paid for. We must accept the fact that this is one of God's great promises to those who believe and accept. We must go from there and sin no more, as He told so many in His Word.

The boys prayed, then I prayed and felt as if two young men began an entirely new life that night, with Jesus Christ at the helm. I pray so.

28

Rise Up, Ye Saints, and Let Us Go

Rise up, ye saints, and let us go
There are many out there that need to know
Some profitable answers from the Senior saints
There are too many bogged down with can'ts and ain'ts.

There is much to say that only you can tell
So, don't clam up and crawl into your shell
Others are struggling because they don't know
So, if we will tell them, we both will grow.

There is a tough world out there they must go through
How you pulled through the dry years, no one knew
But you sailed on and on, and now you are on top
Loaded with experience and wisdom, and this is no
    place to stop.

Many look to the Rocker as the goal of their life
And sit and rock, both day and night
With nothing to do, and nothing to share
Just rub our feet and comb our hair.

RISE UP, YE SAINTS, AND LET US GO

When the day is passed and we can't see the sun
We look for the fruit from the day and there is none
This makes a hard bed, and the night is long
We arise in the morning with a moan and a groan.

We feel of ourselves, and we find many ills
And run to the doctor, and get some more pills.
Run back to the old rocker to sit and to rock
To grumble and gripe, because no one will stop.

No, this is not really what God had in His mind
Led us through the valley to sit in a chair and whine?
Great things we are prepared for, these are our special years
A time for the rejoicing and no room for the tears.

We cannot sit and say that we have no choice
So let us rise up and say in a cheerful voice
I have learned many lessons stored away in my book
To warn the children, to prevent being a crook.

The experiences you have don't have a price
So swap them to others, they think it's nice
Sometime you must travel or go a few miles
But it's worth it all to see some new smiles.

So when you hear someone say "Will you go?"
Always say, "Yes, I will!" and never say "No!"
Think of all the good people like you to meet
So smile, and tell others, as you soak your feet.

The Senior Saints are now on the move,
For much fun and pleasure if you stay in the groove
But if you refuse to go and just sit in your chair
You will soon be like others that don't seem to care.

A HOBO'S JOURNEY TOWARD GLORY

We all will say that God is good
But have we done for Him all that we could
As God blesses us with another day
He expects us to use it and make it pay.

We may not be able to eat and to travel in style
And never know the value of a sincere smile
Just a few words of comfort and cheer
Is sweet music to many that are traveling in fear.

So, let us be ready, faithful and true
You may be called for something to do
Don't shirk and look for a way out
If you do this, you have lost the bout.

When we wear out and reach the end of our trail
We will hear our Lord say that you did not fail.
Your testimony rang out to many, loud and strong,
Cheered up many believers and kept many from wrong.

"You have a paycheck here, so come on home!"
Those you have taught can answer the phone.
Your life has not been of sadness and gloom
For saints like you I have plenty of room.

29

ISAIAH 48:10 • PROVERBS 3:12

Just Sid

Draw a little closer, there is a man I want to tell you
about
He was not only a great man, but was an Indian scout.
Everyone that ever knew him always called him Sid.
Maybe we should have called him something else, but no
one ever did.

When asked where he was born, he would say just some-
place north of Cheyenne.
He had heard someone say that his dad was an Irishman.
The mother of Sid was an Indian squaw,
But gave him away before he could know.

No one knew of Sid ever attending school
The whip and the lariat were his only tools.
Raised to a young boy by an Indian tribe,
Learning to master the rope, and horses to ride.

He left the cold north in the spring of 1885
He followed a wagon train south to stay alive.

They fed and kept Sid, for the language he spoke,
To trade and cheat Indians when they became broke.
The law of the West was do as you can
And if you survived, you stayed in the band.

It was in the hot deserts of Arizona that Sid was dropped
The others made it into Mexico before they were
    stopped.
Sid made his home in an old gold mine.
The water was nearby, but his food was to find.

An old prospector took Sid under his arm
To teach him a new language that did him no harm.
They would not see any pass for weeks at a time
But Sid was riding far out at the age of nine.

Sid's life changed when he reached his teens
The friends that he knew were tough and mean.
They all signed up to move cattle toward the North.
The track was long and hot, and the time was short.

Much Indian Country where they had to ride,
When the Crow Indian prowled, there was no place to
    hide.
Sid knew their languages very plain and clear
When he led the cattle drive, there was much less to fear.

Names like Cody, Wild Bill and others of the West.
Sid knew them all, and said they were the best.
There was not a horse that was too tough for Sid
To break them and train them when he was a kid.
When their spirit was broken and they saw the light,
They would ride much better, and wouldn't kick or bite.

JUST SID

He rode the meanest horses that any man could find
From the Canadian border to the Mexican line.
Using his whip he could remove the head of a snake
While riding his pony at his fastest gait.

The tricks Sid did on his horse with a lariat rope
Cowboys came from far and near, but none could cope.
It was known to the Indians and cowboys the same
That Sid was the best, that won him much fame.

From the countries in Europe, he heard the loud call
To come to England, and they would fill the big hall.
Made many long trips, across the ocean he rode,
Won many friends and beautiful horses he sold.

He performed before presidents, princes and queens
Their cheers and their gifts proved he was the greatest
    they had seen.
On the outskirts of Tombstone is where Sid would live
A quaint little house that rests in the hills.

Hollywood came to Sid for movies to make
Many were made just outside of his gate.
If visiting there now there are many stagecoaches at rest.
The large hill behind his house that Sid loved the best.

He had many good hours listening to the Bald Eagle squall
Would climb many times to answer his Great Father's
    call.
Sid always served his Great Father and served him well
The promise of his new home, he loved to tell.

One hot day Sid struggled and struggled to the top
God told him that climbing in his pain would have to stop.

It was not like Moses, where nobody was found,
But Sid's dark leathery hide was left there on the ground.

There is more that I want you to know
To search our lives and see where to go.
Here was a half-breed that was thrown in a can
Who made a wonderful life, a very good man.

God called him home to rope and to ride.
He needed men like Sid to sit at his side.
God said I need you now, I can't wait any more.
So He took Sid home at the age of one hundred and
    four.

(This is all true. I left Sid in 1983 approximately nine miles
northwest of Tombstone, Arizona, and he died in the spring of
1985. These words were assembled to help encourage many,
many young people giving up on life. I pray many have been
saved by this.)

30

ISAIAH 40:31 • HEBREWS 12:1 • 1 CORINTHIANS 9:24

Running the Race

D ad, I wish you would do something for me since you are going to Lansing early in the morning and have plenty of room in your car."

"Sure," was the reply, "I'll be glad to, what can I do?"

Wayne answered, "Take twelve birds for me there and turn them loose at 8:00 sharp tomorrow morning."

These homing pigeons had been fascinating to me ever since my boyhood days sitting in the cool of an old, open well shelter in Alabama. I will always remember the World War I soldiers telling of times when it could be life or death, trapped in the trenches behind German lines, and how turning a pigeon loose, with a note attached to his leg, carried the important news to the Army headquarters. These stories impressed me then and still do today. Many, many lives were saved by using this method of communication during those dark days. Those tough, well-trained birds had to travel through the most dangerous situations. In Hebrews 12:1,2, the Apostle Paul says that we, as Christians, are definitely in a race, and there is also a large group of spectators. Yes, it is surely a tough course.

Wayne gave me complete instructions concerning the homing pigeons and what to expect. I thought the entire training program was relevant to a newborn Christian. The pitfalls and the remedies would be the same.

As I sat in the parking lot in Lansing, Michigan, awaiting the specified time to free the birds, a group of interested spectators seriously watched, asking many questions of what if, and how long.

A large rabbit hawk sat over in a nearby tree. There were no leaves on this tree, and his vision was clear. The number one question was, "Will he get those young birds when I release them?" "Yes," I answered, "if the young bird fails to rise above or evade the attack, he is a loser. He will definitely be caught and devoured by the hawk." The same happens as a young Christian, if we lurk around with the filth that Satan has provided so plentifully for us, we will definitely be destroyed. We must rise above all questionable acts and places in this life.

When I loosened them, the birds sailed fast and high. The big hawk watched carefully, but saw that his chances to catch those birds were absent. These birds had passed their first hurdle in the race by fleeing from potential trouble.

Some of the birds just circled the large building under construction, and decided to stop and view their surroundings. They perched there for most of the day. Likewise, there are a large number of Christians who use a lifetime and never feel committed to anything. They never put any time or effort into the all-important race that Paul tells us is so vital. He says we must keep struggling ahead with our eyes fixed on Jesus Christ, the ultimate goal. There are far too many just sitting on the rails of life, watching others as they run the race.

Some of the pigeons shot up and out, made the circle over the area twice to be assured of their proper directions, and headed for home.

The following weekend, I asked Wayne, "The General," how the birds did on Monday from Lansing. The answer came back loud and clear. "Bad, bad! All came home, but they had a poor time. They spent all day just fooling around." The Great Master kept mumbling, "Just fooling around."

My lack of knowledge caused a question to pop out: "Can anything be done for them, or will we be eating pigeon stew tonight?"

Wayne very patiently turned to me and explained, "Yes, I will feed them high protein food and give them daily exercise. They will develop into strong secure birds and I have confidence that I will be proud of them in the big race this fall."

It struck me that a struggling Christian, weak and mixed-up in this life, must have a diet of the Word of God. We must feast on this Bible for power and guidance. The high protein food is our only hope. It is motivating to a Christian. The effect of this diet is positive and powerful. We must feast daily on God's Word or we will stay weak and worthless.

Daily exercise is also necessary for a Christian in this race of life. A talk daily to someone about Jesus Christ, keeps us spiritually healthy and strong. We cannot sit in our "coop" and expect to come out strong and ready to go, to face the forces of Satan that dominate this world. We *must* exercise daily on the testimonies and the Word of God to run this race.

A few days later, I was having dinner at Wayne's home and he asked me to go with him to the backyard. We walked to the large, well-arranged pigeon coop that rested within some tall pine trees. The Great Master of Birds suggested that I stand in the open and watch. As he opened the cage, out shot twelve beautiful pigeons. It seemed as though a streak was all I saw pass. The power that filled those birds made them travel at top speed with full confidence. They would fly straight upward and then suddenly level off at the treetops and snap their wings with a noise as loud as a rifle shot. I was amazed as I watched and I was reminded that when a Christian is truly prepared for this great race, he knows no fear. *Confidence prevails!* Knowing that in Christ Jesus we have it all.

Wayne told me that the big race for the championship was from Chattanooga, Tennessee, 650 miles away, and he knew his birds were ready! A verse of scripture flipped before me—John 15:16. Christ told His disciples, "you have not chosen me, but I have chosen you to bring forth fruit, *and you are ready*" (emphasis added).

The race was set. 10,000 birds left Michigan for Chattanooga to be released. All birds were to be loosed at the same split second so each would have an equal and fair chance. Yes, we all have the same source of power, the same Holy Spirit to help guide and direct. If we fail to snap our wings, it's because of our lack of feed, and that we failed to exercise.

The race was through storms; hawks, owls, eagles, and all evil forces were along the path to distract and devour. Some of the birds came along well in the race, but near Ft. Wayne, Indiana, they glided off to the east, heading toward Flint, Michigan. Sadly, the Muskegon birds were following the wrong crowd. We, also, are caught doing this far too many times. We are *individuals* with special souls and we run our own race.

Some birds came home with mud on their feet. Wayne mumbled and grumbled that good birds don't just play around. Their eyes and aim should be toward that cage and that switch on the door which says they have made the arrival home.

Some birds ran the 650 miles and then just landed in the top of the trees to watch, not registering in as the directions requested. Many Christians do the same. They run a good race for a while, but then they just sit on a nearby perch, watching. There are far too many senior citizens that should still be in the race, but are sitting on the fence, never completing the final lap of the race. Instead, they sit comfortably, like wise old owls, just watching others run. Yes, we are still in the race until home is reached.

When the time was checked out by the authorities and all the pigeons' times were recorded, there was a shouting and rejoicing at Wayne's dwelling. It was a very happy day for all, for a winner had been developed. "GREAT!" The winner was home, all trials and troubles were rewarded one hundred times. This bird was retired immediately to special food, a special perch, and attention for the rest of his days. The photographers came from far and near to take the great bird's picture.

The Master knows His sheep and they know Him. A few days after the race a bird was sent by air mail to Wayne. This bird had a broken leg which had been mended by a good bird lover some place in Kentucky. Wayne suggested that the bird had probably blown into a power line or received a blow from a hailstone. Through the Providence of God, the bird was rescued by a Good Samaritan, his wound was bandaged and he was sent to his destination. The band on the bird's leg gave the proper information, just as our names are written in the Lamb's Book of Life. On the bird's arrival home, he was praised and placed side by side with the great champion. Yes, God knows how we are running the race.

31

ISAIAH 41:6 • MATTHEW 10:42 • 2 TIMOTHY 1:16-17

Hold My Hand
or Else I Die

I don't need you, or anyone else to help me!" We have heard these words far too many times, knowing there is no truth in them. The Army general shouts, "Together we live and separate we all die." The company's leader pleads to the complete personnel, "If we don't all pull together we will surely sink."

The Bible tells us, in many places, that as a church we must all cling together. Yes, we as Christians must support one another, or else we fall. There are times in each of our lives when we need help to lift us up and sustain us through various crises.

The young babe that does not have strength to turn the body, needs help. The teen-ager that is struggling in school and cannot cope with the everyday problems that Satan has placed in the path, needs help. The future for them looks so dark and impossible to travel, but these dear souls need someone to point to the light at the end of the tunnel. Many truths that are so vital to their future must be shared with them so that they can grasp them.

Married couples who started with potentially good marriages begin to look like shattered shambles. All has fallen apart and seems to be dividing still farther apart. Bewildered children trying to cope with impossible home problems and school problems, suffer far more than anyone realizes.

The old man that has endured many years under severe hardships has no one to sit and talk with, no one to reach for his hand and guide him to a warm meal and a cozy bed. The little old lady who is dwindling away, losing all her pride and self-respect, has no one to bring her a sandwich or soup, no one to stop by for a few minutes to deposit a few cheerful and encouraging words that may bring comfort and maybe win a smile.

How an we so glibly pass these desperate needs, every day of our lives? Has our society hardened us so that even the words of Jesus Christ are not meaningful anymore? I fear that Christians look for escape routes to evade these all important issues in life, but the need grows greater and greater. We desperately need one another.

God has established throughout all His creation that we cannot make it alone. The honeybees that have been so plentiful and popular since the Pharaohs' time in Egypt, cling together to maintain survival. The more that gather together, the stronger they become. Those clusters of bees can withstand some brutal Michigan winters by "holding hands" and clinging close together.

I was riding out a flood in Louisiana, when this all important issue was magnified to me again. The terrible fire ants which can be so harmful to people, cattle, and crops were having a great year. I heard of young calves and cows being killed by the ants' poisonous stings. I had proudly stated that one good thing about the flooding rivers and streams would be that the fire ants would drown and be washed into the Gulf.

Not so! As I loaded into a small boat, with my rifle, looking for snakes and alligators, the many miles of backwater from rivers were covered and I was amazed to see large clusters of fire ants in the water. Some bunches were three feet across and two feet high, clinging together in a big ball. Each one holding on to the other, as they floated from place to place. Even they knew the only way for their survival was to support one another. I watched them as they would approach a large tree or a dry mound and saw how soon they would all separate and be on their own again.

God's plan is clear that we with good hands, must reach out to others' hands that misfortune has touched. Jesus told His followers that where they had done this "to the least of these, My brethren, so have you done it unto Me." So, if we choose a full and abundant life as a Christian, we must also show compassion and concern to others.

When the winter storms arrive in Michigan and the outside is completely covered with snow, it can be a beautiful scene. Only God can paint this picture. I must relate a lesson God showed me a few years ago, as I walked through three acres of tall pine trees behind our house. The soft, fluffy snow covered the whole area as a solid roof. The heavy snow rested atop the trees. This was a beautiful sight to see as I walked under it all. Only God could have made this possible. The weak branches leaned over and rested on the stronger ones and the treetops bowed into nearby ones for support. The outer edge of the forest, where the trees had no support, was broken down, the trees bowed to the ground. These treetops failed under such a great pressure. Likewise, a Christian cannot face life's pressures alone.

When Christians fail to see the value of fellowship with other Christians, it is sad. Trouble can, and does arise, that will break or deform a life. Many times in my life, someone has come to my rescue and turned me from a path that led to jails and prisons.

We must let our lives touch others with a true concern and love. Take time to stop and show an earnest compassion and help to the teen-ager, who is only an adult in stature. Perhaps only you can help the rapidly crumbling marriage next door. A few right words and serious prayers across a coffee table, may knit a beautiful and loving home together, where children will be raised to a full, pleasant, and useful life.

There are far too many elders out there who are hungry to talk to someone. If only we would loan them an ear for a few hours a week, it could change them from grumpy to happy people. This is not much, just a suggestion, but a must for a Christian. Let us work harder to hold out our hand to the many silent cries.

32

A Total Faith

L et him up, Rufus. That will be enough to mark Siangar
through his life. Everyone that looks at him will know that
he belongs to the devil." Siangar's dad and older brother had
held this 8-year-old boy down and cut his face up with the ends
of a stick. Then they filled the cuts with dirt from a nearby field,
causing large ugly scars that had lasted Siangar throughout his
30 years of life.

The country of Chad is located in the heart of Africa—a
country in much turmoil. Many wars and leadership turnovers
have cursed this land. This could be a great country if partially
developed, but the radical leaders have killed without a cause in
order to keep the population subdued and hungry.

Earl and Shirley went to this land as missionaries, to pro-
claim the Good News of Jesus Christ. They preached the saving
grace that belonged to the black people of Chad in their own
language. Siangar was a young man who listened to the Good
News and was gloriously saved from the devil that he had been
destined to worship, to "a new life" in a living Savior. This
caused much confusion within his family.

The village where Siangar lived had very few believers in it. But by walking through two other villages to where his Christian uncle lived, he could enjoy fellowship. It was a thrilling part of their lives to meet and study and praise God together. Siangar had no other relative who accepted him at all. He was ridiculed by the entire village for his stand for Jesus Christ.

But, his faith never faltered.

One day Earl told Siangar, "If you ever get a chance to go to America, be sure to go to Holland, Michigan. Christ has followers there that would love you greatly, and you would be richly blessed."

Through the great providence of God, this day came to Siangar. He and his interpreters emerged from a big plane in Grand Rapids, Michigan. One of the greatest blessings for my wife and me, was to have all three of them in our home for several days. How thrilled I was when I first saw the smile on that black face, and the white teeth shining like pearls. But the nasty scars that ran down his face made my heart sick. My heart cried out, as I heard his story, but my heart rejoiced and praised God that Siangar's body was only temporary. That beautiful smile out-shined all scars on his face.

Siangar loved life and feasted on Christian love. He loved America: the food, the people and especially, the ice cream. The interpreters that came to America with him had told him that some of his habits must change while he was here; that there were certain foods that he could not eat too much of, that he would sleep only at night, and that he must keep his body clean, taking baths regularly. Siangar had been well taught for his trip to America. He asked many questions about the big buildings, the fast elevators, and many other mysteries of the trip.

The time came for Siangar to meet his former classmate in Washington, D.C. This friend had advanced to become the President of Chad. President and Mrs. Lyndon Johnson were honoring the country of Chad, by having its president to dinner at the White House as their guest. Since Siangar was here in the States, he was also invited.

The trip and his treatment in Washington was a dream come true for this dear one. We would talk of how God had blessed and prospered America and of how people and nations that refused Jesus Christ suffered in so many different ways. We named many nations suffering from disease, hunger and constant fear because Christ was not honored.

Well, the departure date for Siangar's return to Africa came. He was ready to go; ready to return to the village from which he was born and tell the people of things he had learned about his great God. I had many questions to ask of this dear saint of God. We marvelled that I could have Jesus Christ in my heart here 7,000 miles from Chad, and he could have the same Jesus. We agreed that we have a great God. We both recognized, again, the All Knowing, All Powerful, All Caring God.

I recorded Siangar's final day here in America, on tape. How thrilling it was for me to have had the privilege of feasting on the riches of God with a black man from the heart of Africa. I felt all the week that I was walking this earth with the Apostle Paul.

Siangar wanted to return to his people. He had many personal experiences to relate to them. "Maybe," he kept saying, "I can get my dad and brother to accept Jesus." He knew well the uncertainty of his life as a Christian in the land of Chad. He was different and unpopular with the leaders in the village.

Siangar returned to his native country with many exciting testimonies of what he had seen and learned, but it was as in the days of Jesus Christ. Some refused to believe because they chose not to do so. Far too many natives refused Siangar and his Lord completely.

Within one year of his return, another uprising began. The country was destroying all that showed signs of Christian civilization. One sad day we received word that our dear friend was a first martyr for Christ in this turmoil, and that he had been buried in a hole that he was forced to dig. Siangar was buried alive, upside down, for making a solid stand for Jesus Christ before a soldier.

Yes, it was a sad time for several hours in our home, but we were refreshed again in knowing that Siangar's name is written in the Lamb's Book of Life. This dear saint is now at Home, after a life of total faith in Jesus Christ.

33

Heaven's Grocery Store

I was walking down life's highway a long time ago.
One day I saw a sign that read HEAVEN'S GROCERY
STORE.
I got a little closer, the door came open wide.
When I came to myself, I was standing inside.

I saw a host of Angels. They were standing everywhere.
One handed me a basket and said, "My child, shop with
care."
Everything a Christian needed was in that grocery store.
And all you couldn't carry, you could come back the
next day for more.

First I got some PATIENCE, LOVE was in the same row.
Further down was UNDERSTANDING, you need that
everywhere you go.
I got a box or two of WISDOM, a box or two of FAITH.
I just couldn't miss the Holy Ghost for it was all over the
place.

I stopped to get some STRENGTH and COURAGE to
   help me run this race.
By then my basket was getting full, but I remembered
   that I needed GRACE.
I didn't forget SALVATION, for Salvation, that was free.
So I tried to get enough of that to save both you and me.

Then I started up to the counter to pay my grocery bill,
For I thought that I had everything to do my Master's
   will.
As I went up the aisle I saw PRAYER and just had to put
   that in,
For I knew when I stepped outside I would run right
   into sin.

PEACE and JOY were plentiful, they were on the last
   shelf.
SONGS and PRAISES were hanging near so I just helped
   myself.
Then I said to the Angel, "How much now do I owe?"
He said, "My child, Jesus paid your bill a long time ago."

—Author unknown

34

ROMANS 7:23 • ISAIAH 65:21

Freeze

When you hear of someone freezing, what do you first think of? Yes, a police whistle or call, or someone suffering in the cold and severe weather that we so often see during the winters of the Northern states. Let me tell you of another kind of freezing.

As steel workers, spending much time working on dangerous steel columns and walking the beams, we do find fear. Sometimes, we have men "freeze to the steel." I want to relate a time when I saw this happen. The older steel men always told me, as a young man, that when I saw this incident happen, the only remedy was to tie the man off for safety and then take a wrench or hammer and break his fingers or arms to free him from this death hold.

It can happen to good, clean and sensible men on frightening jobs. I was in Birmingham, Alabama on a job setting steel for the new post office building. I did not know any of the men there, so no one knew me either.

I knew this was a tough company to work for. The bosses either liked you or didn't like you. I walked up to this new boss, and he asked me if I was a steel worker. I answered, "Yes, one of the best."

He said, "Can you climb a column of steel?"

I said, "yes." He gave me a coil of 3/4" rope approximately 150 feet long and told me to climb a long, skinny column standing alone. I started up the column to about 35 feet, and he hollered for me to stop and drop him the end of the rope. I locked inside the column with my legs in order to free my arms and shoulders, and dropped him the end of the line. He took it and hung himself to it. He weighed approximately 200 pounds and since only a good steel worker could do this act, he knew I had the experience for the work there. This was my personal interview and I had passed. So, the work began.

I was connecting in the air with a young man just discharged from the Navy—a young man who surely wanted to make good, but knew his experience was limited. We were to climb up the column, side by side, approximately 20 feet apart to change some ropes on top. Our location allowed us to talk to each other, but he did not talk to me or answer questions to our advantage. I knew something was wrong. So, I completed my part of the operation and waited on him. All I could hear was, "I'll get it, I'll get it, I'll get it," and a continued repeat. But, he was not gaining on his assignment, only clinging to the column. He kept repeating, "I'll get it, I'll get it." The grim, determined look on his face showed me he was exhausted. He had done all he could. He had frozen to the steel. I went down my columns, crossed over on the lower beam and climbed up the column he was hanging on.

I kept talking to him. "Let me help you," I said and I encouraged him about how well he had done so far. "Just slide down on my shoulder and we will both go down to the next beam and rest," I said. If the old man said anything to him, I told him, we would both leave the job together. "Just trust me." After approximately ten minutes of this, he grunted and released to my right shoulder. We both slid gently down the column to safety. He was never rebuked about this by anyone, so we stayed on the job.

This has made me consider the power of the mind. Isaiah 26:3 says to be carnally minded is death, but to be spiritually minded is life and peace. First Peter 1:13 says to gird up the loins of your mind.

It seems that our mind controls every part of us. So, let us keep our minds clean and pure, and it will make us much stronger in all things.

35

LUKE 12:42 • 1 CORINTHIANS 4:2

The Scrap Yard Job

There was a very good and interesting job coming up at Padnos Scrap Yards. I was informed of this opening, but this man did not want union men on his job. This man is a very prominent businessman in Holland and I understood his thinking, but I was asked to go and talk to him about this job. The job required a process to convert old scrap cars into small ingots of steel. It takes several steps to produce this and at this time, there were only three places in America where this was done. The major machine was made in Germany and most of the necessary processes were made out of scrap material from the large scrap yard. This I loved to do as it was very interesting to me.

I went in to talk to this man. He was of a prosperous Jewish heritage, but this made no difference in my thinking and conversation. We wholeheartedly agreed that he wanted no one telling him what to do with his money. I told him that if I was instructed to do this job, I would not let any trouble happen. I would select all good men and knew to hire from the Union Hall. If he had anything he did not like, he could come to me and it would be corrected. He agreed and I selected good men,

103

good mechanics, good personalities, and explained the situation to each of them.

The job was a great pleasure for us all. Things ran so smoothly and the owner enjoyed being with the men and watching the various operations.

One day, he and I were talking about his business. The shipping of scrap metal to Israel was almost impossible. He said it would catch on fire while in transit, but the new ingots we were preparing would be the answer. Plus, he could ship more pure metal that was easier to handle. Our relationship was then, and still is, great. One day, as we sat together in a small rail talking, he turned to me and said, "Red, you are a believer, are you not?" I plainly stated that I honestly believe the only way that I, or he, will get into heaven will be through Jesus Christ and that I have no doubts whatsoever. He appreciated my conviction. He and I never had any relationship damage at all. Our friendship became stronger and we were more free to talk about spiritual things as our lives were drawn closer. Israel was a good subject to his whole family, and since I have much love for his country and I understand much of its past heritage, our fellowship remains sweet and open.

We should never try to apologize for what God has said. Study His Word and believe. Be eager to tell others of what has happened in your life.

36

ROMANS 11:1 • 2 KINGS 14:26

Israel #1

My first trip to Israel in the year of 1970 was a test of courage, faith, and a strong desire to see and walk the country in which Jesus Christ had made footprints. I prepared myself in God's Word, in history, geography and the culture of the Bible times for months in advance. This made me more determined to go, and to grasp mentally all that was possible.

This was soon after the Six Day War, which I had followed as closely as possible with news, mail, etc. I knew we were entering a troubled world. First, we flew to Rome, Italy. As we circled the city and airport, I was so full of knowledge and zeal that I counted the seven mountains around Rome. We soon left Rome for Athens, Greece. There, I met a friend from a large crane company in South Africa who was going to Iran and was dreading it.

Our group flew on to Egypt. Cairo was a large, scattered city, and the airport was 16 miles from downtown. But, circling the airport, I took pictures of pyramids, the sphinx, the River Nile, and desert land spotted with wrecked guns, tanks, and army trucks from the final battle of the Six Day War just outside the city of Cairo.

I was amazed at the damage done close to Egypt's largest city. We were not supposed to take pictures of that area from the air, and were asked not to photograph any scenes or objects damaged due to the war. While we were there, we stayed on the River Nile at the Hilton Hotel. From our window, I could see three bridges across the Nile River that had been bombed and were impossible to cross. The Egyptian Museum had holes in the ceilings as large as four feet across, that had not been patched or fixed up. Many bad signs were still left visible.

When we left Cairo, we flew to Beirut, Lebanon, a very large and troubled city. Many faithful Christians were there and one night, we were invited from the hotel to visit with a group of Christians meeting in a woman's home. This group met regularly every month. They were from very poor situations, mostly children and older women. Three of our group were selected to go there on that dark and rainy night. They came for us in a very old wreck of a Jeep, but I shall never forget the praying and singing in all languages, some crying and praising God. We all gave testimonies of what God meant in our lives. They did not want us to leave, so we went back to sing, pray and cry. I will never forget the way in which God met with this group of approximately thirty people of all kinds and ages.

Sadly, these people knew what the future held for them. Yes, death was certain to that area of Beirut, Lebanon within six months. I was privileged to realize, as Paul had, that living for Christ is not always cheap. I saw this area destroyed on TV soon after our trip home.

We left Beirut for Baal Bek Valley, "the home of Baal gods fold." The Syrian army was gathered. My, what a great treat for me to see and study the oldest city left for men to view.

To enter Israel from a neutral country, we had to go to the Island of Cypress, landing in Nicosia. Barnabas, a fellow traveler of Paul, had lived in this city in Paul's day. I loved that island, occupied by Greeks and Turks.

Israel was still being bombed. A woman from Grandville, Michigan was shot and killed while we were on Cypress and no one wanted to come out and get us. Finally, a small El Al airplane came for us. *Everything* was inspected before we could leave the airport, even my shaving bag. Everything had to be laid out on the ground where the pilot and co-pilot could look at and feel it. They would not take two people from the same family on the same flight, such as brother and brother, dad and son, etc. My roommate from Indianapolis went first and I was glad to see him at our hotel in Jerusalem two days later. We traveled in a bus with both an Arab driver and a Jewish driver for when we entered an Arab danger zone. The right driver would get behind the wheel as the other went back and laid under the back seat to hide while the bus was unloaded and searched. This worked out well for all of us and we all survived the trip.

In Jerusalem, the place I most desired to see and visit if possible was Calvary. This desire was granted one Sunday morning, just about daybreak, for me and two other men. We walked on a very narrow road up a steep grade that was not wide enough for cars and trucks to travel. At the top was a small hut to house the guard from the rain. A man was there alone and in a deep stupor. I woke him up, and we all gave him half an American dollar. He let us pass by and was happy.

There is a Jewish cemetery on top of Calvary mountain. On the end toward Jerusalem City, a rugged jet of mountain projects out. Under this, on the ragged end, the image of a skull can be seen. The eye sockets, nose and mouth point toward the city. This was, and still is, called Golgotha, "the place of the skull." As I stood there above the skull, I looked up, and it seemed to me that this was as close to heaven as I had ever been. Even though my life had been on tall buildings, towers, etc., never had I felt so close to heaven. I saw Mount Moriah where Abraham had offered Isaac on an altar as God had requested him to do. Then across God's city was the place of the last offering, where the blood of Jesus Christ was spilled for the sins of this wicked world. I saw it all. Yes, and my heart was blessed by it all.

The grave where the body of Christ was placed was not only a sacred spot, but it seemed as if the Bible came bursting open before me there. The total picture of the geographic location of Calvary, Gethsemane, and the grave was proven so real and true. As much as I had heard and read of Christ's tomb, I was not prepared to see that the right end of Christ's tomb was approximately 6 inches longer and very roughly hewn out, even though the rest of the grave was as smooth as silk clothes. Why? We walked outside into the garden area and I remarked that this was a borrowed grave, as Christ was a normal size for a Jew. But when the crucifixion atop Calvary took place on the cross, the Bible states that every joint in His body was unloosed. So, this is why the women that fateful day had a longer body to work with. This was when the rough or I say "war finish" was done to make room for the body of our Savior. Another lesson to show me, again, the flawless truth of God's Word.

37

PROVERBS 4:18

Important to Whom?

I was a young, married man with one of the greatest families a man could possibly have. Yes, I loved them very much. But, one day, I was shown by our living God some important mistakes I was making in my very important plans. I pray that whoever or wherever you are, you will think on this parable.

I was working in New Orleans on a good construction job, making a decent amount of money and working a lot of hours. In Gadsden, Alabama were my wife and two girls and a young son, Ben. My work schedule forced me to work several weekends and not to make those trips to Gadsden very frequently, even though I wanted to do so. I was working for no other cause— only to provide for my wife and children.

We soon had a new son born, David. David was approximately six months old when a local policeman came to my job to tell me that if I wanted to see my son alive, I had better get home, and soon. David was dying of bronchial pneumonia. I thought of my dear wife and all the troubles she had and the decisions she was compelled to make without her husband.

I immediately left for Gadsden, 380 miles away. Along the way, I cried and prayed, asking for God's forgiveness. I promised

God that if He would spare David's life, I would be a faithful father by my family's side. Well, God saved David from that selfish act of his father, and when I left Gadsden to return to the job in New Orleans, my whole family was with me. Sometimes, it seemed humanly impossible to meet these many jobs and stay together as a family, but God always managed it for us. How faithful He has been and how selfish we sometimes are, trying to do what we think God wants us to do. When we are truly in God's will, we know it. Money is not the primary object as we so often think.

These troubles and changes have made us all closer, stronger Christians, more dependent on our Lord's leading and the truth of His promises. And it is just great to be living on the Lord's side of life. We have met and sung praises with so many great people that we would never have met if I would have had my selfish and struggling life.

Dave has proven never to be a trouble to us. He has been a good child and good student, a special treasure from God even to this day, and a strong warrior for our Lord. We can never give enough thanks to God for whipping me into a sensible man.

38

EPHESIANS 2:8-9

You Go First, Herschel

This is not what we really meant from the top of a large smokestack at Port Sheldon Powerhouse. We were building a large smokestack higher and higher. Herschel and I were working the top as we extended the stack upward seven and a half feet each day. At this time, we were up 135 feet and still going upward.

Inside the stack, it was getting darker and darker each day as the vision downward was dimmed more all the time. We had to drop down a few feet each day in order to move materials up in preparation for the setting up of the next seven and a half foot section.

Herschel and I had talked about life during the first part of that fatal morning. Yes, total life—how some decisions we had made were bad, and how some were wonderful. Herschel had a wonderful wife and a five-year-old daughter and they all lived on a large ranch with his father-in-law, in Livingston, Alabama.

Herschel had one bad eye that was very noticeable to all, and as we talked on this particular morning, he told me that there was a doctor in Memphis who was going to fix his eye when they returned to that area for the Christmas season. He and his wife had figured it out just last night, that if he kept working regularly there as he had been, they would have enough money saved for the operation—$1,000 was all the doctor had requested to make his eye good again.

The evening before, they had been to our place and I gave them a washing machine they needed badly in their cottage. So, we were as close as brothers. On construction jobs, because each other's actions at work are so important—many times it's a life or death situation—a solid trust must be built between the workers.

Herschel had told me that his father-in-law wanted him to stay and take over the ranch for him. His last words were, "I wish a thousand times I had." As he climbed down inside the stack, a loose board flew up and Herschel went down, grabbing and sailing, 135 feet to his death. When I reached his body, it was riddled. All his teeth were out, the bone in his thighs went through his shoe soles. Yes, life had left Herschel in a hurry.

It's foolish for me to say that life is uncertain and death is sure, but, it is so. I have seen far too many of these types of endings, and it affects my life in the way that I tell others of how suddenly and surely it can come. So, we must be sure of our eternity. We can prepare for this while we are here and sane. I seldom receive any flack on this subject, because they know that I am sure of what I am speaking about. We must be born into His kingdom, by faith in what Christ has done for us. We must receive this great truth. I say God breathed into us a soul when we were born, and we must check it back in. We are responsible for what we did with it. It must come back in.

39

Hollywood—No

One of the most profitable lessons I have learned was definitely guided by the Holy Spirit. I pray that you will enjoy the true value of this parable.

Louisiana was always a fascinating place to me. The people there lived so free, and yet so honest, so loving and caring. Maybe not all being guided from the Word of God, but so many lessons we learn together.

I was teaching a Sunday school class of sixteen-year-old boys. There were sixteen of them in my class and I felt close to each one of them and their families. We had a great relationship and I was truly respected and favored by all the young men. I wanted to treat the class to a baseball game in New Orleans on a special Saturday afternoon. The New York Yankees and the Pittsburgh Pirates were to play. On the Pittsburgh team was the first player to sign a $100,000 contract—Paul Pettitt.

We all gathered for this special day of importance to all of us, but the day was spoiled by a constant rain. To avoid a total loss, I ventured into the player's dressing room, introducing myself and the sixteen boys. The Pittsburgh manager told me Paul Pettitt was who I should see. Within a few minutes, we were talking to the most popular player in baseball. He sure impressed all of us as a special person. When we left him that day, he gave all the boys a baseball and bat, plus some real words of advice.

We left the dressing room, thrilled at the experience, but having only used approximately forty-five minutes of the evening. I suggested that we go to a Western movie. So, we paid twenty-five cents each to see Fred Thomson in a cowboy movie.

The following day at church, we were still walking on air. I was telling an elder deacon about the day before, which he had already heard about. I related to him the events of the great day and he calmly listened, then asked, should we have gone to the movie? I answered that it was only twenty-five cents each and we had the time to spare, but this did not satisfy the dear saint. He said that we were helping to support the most ungodly organization on the earth. I said, "only a little bit," but I realized then how right he was and that God could not be pleased with me on that note. I had a feeling of guilt. I wanted to be an all-out Christian, but I saw where I had failed. It seems that the Holy Spirit never allowed any bitterness or sharp words from me. So, I told Mr. Johnny that he was right and thanked him for the way he had enlightened me.

Several years later, I made a trip to Israel and Turkey. I traveled as near as possible to Mt. Ararat where Noah's ark is hanging between two mountains. Due to the two governments involved, it is difficult to visit, so we failed to go up to the mountain, only going to Ankary, Turkey. So, interest still lingered in my mind to know more.

A few years later, I was on the deacon board in a local church. At this meeting, we failed to complete all the business. So, another date was being discussed for this cause and the date suggested was when the movie of "Noah's Ark" was in town. I suggested another date and a fellow deacon asked me why. I related to him how I wanted to see this since I had been so near to the ark on my journey. A chilling response came. Art said that he had two teenage daughters, who thought well of me as a strong Christian, and he would not want to hear them say that they had seen Red Farabee going into a movie house. I told Art not to worry about that, I had realized my error and they would not see me entering the movie house. Trust me.

Again, there is nothing more important to me than my living testimony for the Lord and Savior. God expects His church, the Bride, to be spotless as possible. I have been blessed and strengthened spiritually through it all and I do not cater to, or support, Hollywood knowingly. This is truly another lesson learned from an elder, godly Christian, thanks be to God.

40

PROVERBS 21:31 • PROVERBS 29:25

The White Shoes
Went That Way

We were returning home from a visit to a friend's farm one beautiful summer night. The sun had gone down and the dark was beginning to rule. We had our two daughters riding with us in the back seat of our large Oldsmobile. This was a car I feared. I could not understand why its kind were allowed on the roads of this country, when the back door opened from the front. This created a terrible fear that someone, sometime, would pull the opening handle from the inside and the door would fly open in transit. We had just driven through Gadsden, Alabama and were entering the outskirts of the city where the street and traffic lights were dim and few.

Nicaea and Ivol, our two daughters, were dressed up like dolls. Their mother always managed to see to that. Beautiful dresses with fringes, and new shoes with all the trimmings dominated the trip to the farm. The young girls were approximately three and six years of age, sitting very comfortably in the rear seat of that big Oldsmobile.

I was driving approximately thirty-five miles an hour going up an incline, when I felt a gush of air circle my neck. It kept coming and I knew something serious had just happened, so I pulled over as rapidly as possible and stopped. When I asked Nicaea, where was Ivol?, she very calmly answered that she didn't know, but that Ivol's new white shoes just went that way. She pointed to the open door on the left side.

I rushed down the center of the street, waving to stop any traffic that would stop. I was in total shock and could not even visualize anything good coming out of this. But, God intervened. There were two young boys, not even teenage yet, who were walking together toward town and saw Ivol fall from the car. They dared the traffic with their lives to reach Ivol and drag her to safety on the side of the wide street. Ivol was saved from her fall as a miracle happened before our eyes, plus the super brave act of the two black boys. This was one very heroic act that never reached the pages of publicity. I thanked and thanked the boys, and they went on their way, never to be seen again. I have rejoiced so many times in prayers, asking God to be good to those young boys, to bless them greatly and let them know we all had grateful and humble hearts for their unusual feat. Yes, I must say again, angels of our Lord entered our lives clearly and plainly.

To make this act more perplexing, these were the troublesome times of Martin Luther King's marches and race problems were being promoted. Thanks be to God, after a quick trip to the hospital with our daughter, the damages proved to be very minor—only a skin burn on the left forearm and some skin rubbed on her left hip. Ivol was still holding to a joint of the sugarcane a farmer had given her as she entered the car. The white shoes were not as white as when they last passed in front of Nicaea's eyes, but the great humbling effect of these events keeps us praising and giving thanks to our Creator and Keeper, knowing that someway, somehow, He has His angels all around. Glory be to God.

41

EPHESIANS 5:15 • PSALM 104:3

Walk Circumspectly

I was working in Atlanta, Georgia on a very large and dangerous steel job. We were erecting fifteen more stories on an
already existing nine-story telephone company building.
During those years, very little safety was taught or demanded on
construction jobs, especially in Atlanta. We would be swinging
large loads of steel over streets and lots, and raising it to the top
of buildings, handling it like hay. People would be walking
below without even looking up. During my 40 years on high
steel, it bothered me more that I might drop something, or fall
on someone, than that I might fall myself.

I was then friendly with some pilots who flew planes with
targets towed behind for men of the armed forces to practice
shooting at. These new recruits were not always best marksmen,
and since this was when the war was progressing, their tow tar-
get pilots were sometimes shot to the ground. This was not considered important enough to enter the newspapers. Yet, most of
the time these men would use alcohol to settle their nerves
enough to cope with their dangerous jobs.

They would always ask me, how I stayed up on those small
members of steel without falling. What did I think of to manage

this. I had the most dangerous job anyone could have, but I would always try and joke it off saying that if you were hungry enough, and there was a piece of cornbread up there on top, you would sure go and get it. But, not so. When we seriously talked of this dangerous position, I would tell them that when walking steel in the air, I would never lean into the wind. It could not be trusted and my life was at stake. Instead, I would bead my eyes directly on the steel *only*, and see nothing but that beam where I was going to place my feet.

Your walk must be sure and careful—walk as the Apostle Paul says to walk, circumspectly. This can be done. If we look around, or down toward the street below, that is where you will be. Our lives must be directed with our eyes totally on Jesus Christ and the Word of God. When we begin to look at other things, we will surely fall. This is done with much prayer, thought, and determination to commit the task. The faith required for these jobs keeps multiplying and we feel more sure, day by day. We know there is One higher than ourselves, helping us along. I pray that this led many nervous pilots to think seriously about this adventure of life.

42

Real Values

Again, I learned a very important lesson from an older veteran in God's work. I sat by quietly and watched the Word of God in action.

You may not agree with me on this story, but think carefully as you continue to read. We were in the process of paying off a loan on an additional church building program. There was $67,000 left to be paid off after all the methods we could think of of were exhausted. As deacons, we had decided to visit all of our membership and let each one commit themselves to how much and when they could, and would, pay. I was a young and vibrant Christian, full of zeal, and a desire to learn the Word. Mr. J. J. White, the chairman of our deacon board, was very knowledgeable and experienced in the work of our Lord.

We had a man operating the Friendly Bar who had won a twenty-year pin for continuous attendance in the church Sunday school. He ran a very respectable operation and everyone loved Taylor Jones. But, after his return from World War II, he did not attend church for some reason, maybe for no reason, though Mrs. Jones, his wife, was faithful in attendance without her husband. Money within the household was plentiful.

Taylor Jones heard of the program and called Mr. White to state that he would give $5,000 to him if he would come to his place of business and receive it. Mr. White responded by asking to meet him three doors up the street at the bank, at a certain time, to complete the process. Taylor Jones answered back that if Mr. White was ashamed to enter his business place, he would not give the church the $5,000. After several conversations, it boiled down to the fact that God really didn't need Taylor's money but, if he wanted to give it to the Lord's work, he should step forward with it. I was watching with interest to see the outcome of this. I must say, as a young, aggressive, Bible teacher and deacon, I began to feel that it was no big problem and I could go and get the money. But Brother J. J. White held to his conviction that Taylor must give his offering himself. I think maybe Mrs. Taylor brought the money and placed it in a regular offering.

After years of watching and meditating on this issue, which could be considered minor, I saw how God handled it. I must admit, at one time the pupil tried to be smarter than the teacher, but patience and experience changed this.

I was installing a flume on a large channel of water to float paper wood into the big chipper from where it was unloaded. This flume, or open channel of water, divided two areas of the city. One beautiful morning, the plant manager met me at the gate to ask me to get all my men together and cover all areas of the plant with pails in order to gather all the pieces of human we could. Following the big chipper to all conveyors, etc., we gathered all the "man" we could find. We did this with approximately 30 men. I suggested two men to a bucket would gather all pieces of clothes or pieces of bloody chips. When we had completed this process, we had approximately one and a half buckets of human parts. Not knowing who had lost their life that fateful night, all personnel were checked out on all shifts of work and all could be accounted for. Approximately three days later, we learned that a middle-aged man was missing. This man had not been totally mentally fit, but everyone loved him.

He was last seen passing time in Taylor Jones' Bar (the Friendly Bar). No one was concerned about when and how he went home, but to go home, he had to cross the water flume. We gathered that he did not find the crossway we had provided for this crossing and so we never saw our good friend, "Barn," again.

As I kept observing time, it was less than six months later that Mr. Taylor died. He grieved himself to death soon after this event.

I learned another good lesson from all of this. I was made more sure that God is the God of all, and who am I but a small particle of His kingdom. To try to quibble over a few dollars is useless when all belongs to Him. We must learn to separate our wills or wants from His Word and His will. Yes, we should always be found faithful to His Word, and to the ever-present Holy Spirit in our lives. Yet another good lesson learned from a faithful, godly elder.

43

PSALM 25:5 • I CORINTHIANS 3:13

The Preciousness of Every Day Revealed

We were living in Bogalusa, Louisiana while on some steel jobs in that area. As a family, we were sure enjoying this area and these great people. Our children had no problems making friends there and we loved the people, the church, the food and the weather.

One day our six-year-old daughter was bitten by a friend's dog approximately two blocks from our home. Being raised in Alabama, we knew the dangers of what we called, "mad dogs." The temperature and climate conditions in these areas were ideal to cause serious problems such as hydrophobia. Yes, human beings could very easily receive this disease. Then, as we knew, it was a very horrible and certain death. Thankfully, when the dog bit Ivol, we knew the dog. On the day of the bite, I went up to talk to the family who owned the dog. I also checked with the health department as to the hazards and remedies. It was agreed that the dog was to be observed day by day for 21 days.

My workplace was such that I could come by each day from work to carefully review the dog. I would look for any different action, any eye color change, any foam, etc., around the mouth, carefully examining all factors to watch for any suspicious change. If any changes were noticed, our daughter would have to receive eleven shots into her stomach, one each day. This was no sure cure, but it was the only hope we would have.

Each day, my thoughts on the job were to be sure and look the dog over well and pray that there were no new signs.

Then, when I was welcomed at home, the question was, "How was the dog?" Each day carried a big potential of one of our own not having a tomorrow. At night, I would thank God for that day and ask Him for a good day tomorrow. The next day was the same routine—thanking God each day for another great day so we could sleep again. Altogether, this went on for 21 days. Then we rejoiced for His goodness. Let me ask you, should we not be as grateful for each day even if no one has been bitten by a dog? I realize more day by day how fragile our lives are, even when we feel so sure of ourselves.

44

LUKE 14:34

God's Salt Shaker

My Dear, I am not alone here for my Lord is with me night and day in all that I do. We enjoy every hour together. I talk to Him, I sing and laugh with Him. I know anyone that comes up here thinks that I am crazy." These were the words of Grandma Farmer in Varnado, Louisiana.

When we planned to go up to Grandma Farmer's, it was no problem to get the kids tuned up for that. She loved to talk and explain everything thoroughly. She would busy herself watering and talking to each flower, of which she had many of all colors and kinds. She would always have something to serve to us all and anything she prepared was good eating. To roam the small farm was a special treat. The duck, geese, guineas, dogs, etc., never failed to greet their new friend. A good fishing hole only a few feet away supplied fish at a minute's notice. Everything was special. All was a creation from our Lord, placed here so that we could enjoy each thing.

Grandma Farmer had three sons and they all enjoyed a successful family life of their own. It was always a treat for them to return home and enjoy prime time with their mother and home place. This dear soul would never tire of bouncing around her

125

home and yard. The boys would often bring some friend with them as everything was always flavored with Jesus Christ. The Farmer's home had entertained governors, senators, doctors, and even many unfortunate ones for a special day.

Never could anyone leave this place without feeling that they had spent some time in another world where there was a feeling of love, care, and compassion to all things. It seemed as if even the flowers turned their blossoms to face you and smile.

Sometimes maybe the wind would turn a flower blossom down and Mrs. Farmer would stop everything to find some stick or string to tie the flower back to a comfortable position. Even the dogs walking through the yard never stepped on the flowers. It seemed as if all life was precious, and God was there to help Mrs. Farmer care for and enjoy the old home place.

I have often thought if all Christians professing belief, would sprinkle the Christ-like savor as this dear saint did, what a glorious world we would be living in. "This was everyday with Jesus, for real."

One day, when the Lord called Mrs. Farmer to go home with Him, it was just like crawling over into the other wagon. She went home with Jesus.

Yes, this dear woman left such a vacancy there in the Varnado section of Louisiana. Thanks be to God that I had met her.

45

LUKE 24:47

Early Missions

During the early 1940s, I was working on steel buildings in the New Orleans area. Things were very active up and down the Mississippi River. Ships loaded with war material, produce, oil, gas, lumber, and grain were continually going to South or Central America and various ports in Old Mexico on the river front.

There was a mission-like place for the sailors and workers on these ships to go if they were stranded, tired, or just wanted to stop in. The churches in the area would each be regularly scheduled to provide food and a spiritual meeting on certain days. We, from Calvary Baptist Church, had a monthly Sunday to provide this. The women would cook, bake, and provide baskets of food, etc., for the day. I would go and help with the service. Yes, I was in the early thirties of my life, but my experiences were of fifties, so I loved to go and try to talk to these foreigners who liked to stop by sometimes. 150 or 200 men and boys would be there, mostly from Central America. I found it a great joy to tell them of Jesus Christ, our only hope. There always seemed to be someone there to translate, or to pass the good news on. I felt at home and that God was using us there. We would all sing, pray, and eat together and tell stories and experiences of life. It was amazing to see how the name, Jesus Christ, could be so loving, so powerful, and so caring for each one.

Sometimes, our services would run on through from 9:30 a.m. until 10:00 p.m. This was a great experience and training for a young man desiring to do God's will.

I could easily see within my lifetime, then, my early hobo days, my college days, my vocation in steel, my love for people, and the powerful draw of my Lord, all fit together so well. I looked nowhere else for satisfaction. I was a happy and secure-feeling young man. God had provided me with experiences, teachers and power for this cause, thanks to the working of the Holy Spirit.

46

1 JOHN 1:1-7 • 2 TIMOTHY 4:18 • HEBREWS 12:1

Don't Follow the Leaf

For real adventurers, there is no more exciting place than the Pearl River Swamp of Louisiana. I was fortunate enough to spend many seasons there and enjoyed them all. The floods, the snakes, the large spiders, the hungry alligators, and the wild hogs, all kept one's mind and heart racing.

One year, I received news that my grandson and his high school partner were coming to visit with us for several days. I wanted to make their vacation as exciting as possible and I knew they would enjoy fishing in Louisiana's greatest stream, the Pearl River. This would be no trouble for me, because I lived on a canal that flowed into the Pearl River near our place.

Where the Pearl River and the canal met, was a large and unusual falls of approximately forty feet and a good place to view this exciting place was easy to get to. I stood there one day talking to a local resident. We would see dogs, cows, parts of houses and anything else that came down the river go over those falls in full view. This disturbing scene was hard to bear. The man told me that he had once sent an automobile tire down the river to watch it go over the scary falls. Amazingly, he remarked, he came back to view this scene the following day and the tire was still bobbing up and down in the white foam. How awful to think of the results to a human body entering these falls. I could even imagine a terrible hell there eagerly awaiting.

The time came, and our company arrived for a good visit. Yes, we soon had the fishing boat loaded, and three eager fishermen were crossing over to a special location for the big catch. I knew of the dangers that could lie ahead for anyone heading in this direction, but the young and eager could not envision anything but good, clean excitement on this adventure.

As I sat in the boat, my mind was concerned for our safety, so I kept pulling off small twigs or leaves from the brush and tossing them into the river. I would watch the slow movement of the leaf. Sometimes it would even make a little circle in the water and gradually ease off downstream. According to my leaf gauge, we were definitely heading toward serious trouble.

It seemed as if we were moving faster than we had expected, which created a tough problem in trying to pull out from the fast moving current. The motor could not push us out of the danger lane and the paddles were useless to avoid the certain disaster ahead.

I prayed, and we planned our method to try and cope. With motor and paddle all working at full power, we guided the boat to a nearby cypress tree. At high speed, Kevin reached out with his strong arms and grabbed the tree enough to stop us from the fateful disaster. We gathered our wisdom and carefully eased into a way of exit. This I thanked God for many, many times. I thanked Him for His guidance and protection.

I think the major lesson I learned from this adventure was how easily we can be guided off into deep sin. Sometimes, we are sailing along thinking about good times, enjoyment and pleasures, but are very subtly being led into trouble. Sometimes, we never have a second chance in life. I knew there was great danger ahead when I saw the leaf floating faster and faster toward the terrible fate, but excitement, enjoyment, and taking chances took control. We lost our control very soon, and were sailing helplessly into death and eternity. Sin lurks close to these worldly pleasures. The resistance we think we have, fails us. Too late, our destiny is already within the grasp of the evil one. Beware, watch for the leaf's movement. Turn and flee in due time.

47

HEBREWS 6:12

Found—
Holland, Michigan

We had just completed a big steel job in St. Louis, Missouri with no serious accidents, and all were riding high in the main office. The owner, and president of the company, and I were talking of jobs coming up at a later date. Mr. Stocker asked me how I would like to go to Holland, Michigan on a job for General Electric. I asked Mr. Stocker to sit down quietly in that good chair. When he did, I asked him, was he sure Holland was in Michigan? He replied, "Sure, I have been up there—a nice clean town to live in." Little did I know that within a few months I would be riding into Holland, Michigan, but I must say now that Holland has been good for Red Farabee and his family.

We had many customs and traditions to adjust to in Holland. While I was traveling from job to job, we had always located ourselves in as strong a church as we could find. Being of a Baptist background, our first selection was a Baptist church. This may seem strange, since my Granddad was a circuit rider under John Wesley's leadership. His territory was from Knoxville, Tennessee to Gainesville, Georgia. Yes, it was a hard life, and is anytime when Jesus Christ is proclaimed clearly and plainly even today.

My Grandpa died en route to Gainesville one cold winter. Horseback was the mode of transportation from house to house, but somehow he died outside on the road. People can be very cold and indifferent, even so-called Christians.

We visited the First Baptist Church on a Sunday morning in September. It was a small congregation, but no one greeted us us there. Louise said she was not going back there again. I remarked that I had promised God to be used wherever He wanted me and wherever there was the most need, and that place needed help more than any place I had ever been. So, I returned that same night. I heard some woman behind me ask another woman, "Who is that man?"

The other woman said, "I don't know, but he and his family were here this morning." I began to work on this needy and sore place. Soon we began to love the people and cast our lot there, and God blessed us as we worshipped there.

One day, during a revival meeting, there were many souls saved into God's service forever, for the Holy Spirit was working in an unusual way. This I was accustomed to. I went into the small prayer room one night with a young fourteen-year-old boy. I didn't know Russell well, just as a friend of our son, Ben. I referred Russell to many Bible verses and talked with him. We cried, we prayed, and when we left the prayer room, Russell was a new person in Jesus Christ. I had no doubt of his conversion and I was thrilled for him. That Friday night, I could not stop rejoicing for him. I wanted to go the next morning, to be sure his father and mother heard the grand news from the beginning. At that time here in Holland, this was somewhat foreign to people and we were labeled a cult by some of the people in Holland.

Not knowing the family, I drove to Russell's home to meet his mom and dad. His father was a member of the board for Hope College. I repeated to him exactly word for word what had happened. I spoke as a father to a father, about his son. I told him that Russell had been saved last night. He and his good wife rejoiced with me that same Saturday morning and the father thanked me many times.

When my first book came out, this man and I became closer and closer. I was informed regularly of Russell's whereabouts. He became a Baptist minister in California and has a wonderful family, today. God is faithful. A few months ago, I called over to his Mom and Dad's and I said to the Mrs., "You probably don't remember me."

She replied loudly and clearly, "No never, how could I ever forget Red Farabee?" The great importance of being faithful to the teaching of God's Word leads to blessings beyond our imagination. Today, we are not willing to be used and there is no power or fire. This is not due to God's failure or because the Bible is outdated as many try to believe.

48

HEBREWS 9:28

His Appearing

I had often wondered what would happen in our churches if the Apostle Paul was to suddenly walk in, without letting anyone know who he was, or why he was present. Better yet, what if Jesus Christ was to drop in just as our song service began? How would He be received in our churches today?

Well, a few years ago I almost found out part of the answer. On a very beautiful day, a special Sunday, a large crowd was in church for an award presentation. In this church, I was the President of the Men's Brotherhood. We boasted of 100 men faithful to the cause of Christ. We had worked faithfully for a long time, trying to enlarge our ministry. I would meet every new man, trying hard to win them into our membership of believers.

A man walked in, all dressed in white, even his hair was a beautiful white. His coat, tie, pants and shoes were as white as could be. He carried a nice size Hertel Bible in his hand and behind him were two beautiful girls who looked to be in their teen years. They, too, were dressed in beautiful white dresses, white shoes and holding Hertel Bibles. This was very, very unusual as they were total strangers to all. This man stood tall and straight, walking directly to the front of the church and sitting on the second row of pews on the left side. He never stopped or shook hands along the way.

It seemed as if everyone was directly beaded in on those three visitors. Everything they did and every move they made, seemed to be perfect. When the service was dismissed, I went directly to Mr. Smith from some city of West Texas and met him and his daughters. I invited them to have dinner with us that day, but later on this Sunday evening he came to our place in fellowship and prayer. He was the most spiritual person I had ever met. His faith was super strong and his prayers were powerful, straight to heaven. We continued a sweet relationship all the days he was in our city. He would go visiting in homes and went with me to visit in the hospital, always godly in all he said and did. One day, he asked me why the youth director and the other leaders in the church were so eager to flee from his presence. They proved to be too nervous even to speak to the new visitor. This was true of many in our congregation—always running from him, always needing to be elsewhere. Mr. Smith noticed this and asked why? We talked of this, as I knew their lives and families better than he. We could only imagine them to be carnal Christians, not fully committed in their belief and action.

Mr. Smith and his daughters sold Hertel Bibles for living expenses. They did this from home to home and it gave them a great opportunity to give their testimony to many. Meeting this dear family was the richest blessing, to me, of the entire summer. We kept in contact with each other for several years. I am sure this was not the Apostle Paul or Jesus Christ, but I saw many people I had thought of as strong Christians, shudder and disappear without any explanation at the presence of the Smiths.

Are we prepared within our hearts, minds and lives to meet these great people of the Bible? I feel very few would *run to meet* any one of these great Bible characters.

49

LEVITICUS 24:16 • MARK 3:29 • JAMES 2:7

The Unpardonable Sin

I have thought, prayed, studied and read much about this very important and disturbing subject. I have had many opinions and ideas, but I want to relate my experience and knowledge about this. Please read carefully.

I was working on a steel job in Bogalusa, Louisiana and had met many good people. I was well known in that area as a steel superintendent and for my Christian life. Yes, my connection with the Men's Brotherhood launched out to the entire parish. I met a meat cutter by the name of Cooper at a grocery store. I heard he had been saved from his previous life to a new life in Jesus Christ. The following year, I heard that he was preaching in a small church down on the Mississippi Coast. People were being saved and all was great. We would praise God for His wonderful works regularly. Cooper's church was growing rapidly, and he was being mightily used of God.

Approximately two years later, I was sent to Bogalusa to add another addition to a very large paper mill. Soon after my arrival there, I asked around about how Cooper was doing down on the Gulf Coast. This sad note came back to me. Cooper was back in town. He had left his church saying that he had made money and had lots of fun there. He denied any truth that God had used him. He said it was all phony and that there was no truth to these happenings by the Holy Spirit.

Cooper was found in his bed at home dying, but could not speak. His tongue had swollen so large that his mouth could not hold it. He could only roll his eyes and head in order to speak or communicate. This is the only man I ever saw this way in my life.

I see, as I search the scriptures on this subject, that in order to be guillty of this sin, one must give credit or praise to Satan for what the Holy Spirit has done. *This must be spoken:* A denial of the known work of the Holy Spirit and passing the praise on to the devil. Cooper had done this and I saw no other man suffer as he did in his latter days of life. God's Word is true, powerful, inspirational, and fearful. Let us not make a playhouse of God's Word.

50

MATTHEW 5:1-15

Demons of Our Day

On one of our frequent trips to our place in Louisiana, I met a very unusual situation. On our very first day there, I was asked to teach the Sunday school lesson at a new Baptist church on the Varnado Highway. I asked the leader to tell me what the lesson was about and he just told me it was about "demons." I knew then that I had much studying to do. But, the Lord handed me a super lesson already prepared.

The second day there at our location, I was erecting a metal tool house for the lawnmower, etc. We had planned to stay in Bogalusa for approximately two weeks and then travel on West for several weeks. We did not intend to disturb the young couple we had rented our house to. They could remain there for the winter. He was a fine young man with the Sheriff's Department.

Wade and Frielder Burton were working with me on this small building. As we were assembling it, Frielder pulled out his pocketknife to cut a gasket to fit. I made a remark on how sharp it looked, calling it an Alabama boxing glove. We all laughed and Wade remarked, "You should see the one he took off a man a few days ago." I asked questions about the event, and in a few minutes I was holding a fifteen or sixteen inch knife in my hands. It was a very frightening weapon even in its scabbard. He told me the following story, which I recorded.

Wade was called out on a distress call, to a certain bridge out toward Varnado, a nearby city. The problem was a naked man living under the bridge. He would come out jumping and waving as women and children drove by. The man had only this knife strapped around his neck, dangling in mid-air. He had no home known to the police and no record. However, the large knife had been stolen many weeks before. The man was very strong, and resentful of being arrested. The place of arrest was not far from the church in which I was to teach the class on demons the following Sunday.

Wade and I talked of this event at length. We also discussed an arrest, the previous week, of a large black man who was disturbing pedestrians in the heart of downtown. Wade said he approached the man and asked him to go with him. The man refused, reached out and grabbed Wade by the shoulder with one hand, picked him up and turned him around 180 degrees before he put him down. Wade weighs approximately 195 pounds, is six foot, one inch tall, and is in super physical condition. He is as nimble as a cat, but he could not get close to this man. He called for help, and six men were needed to subdue this prisoner. When he was put into the patrol car, the prisoner cursed and cursed loudly, screaming. Then he would quote verses from the Bible for a long time, before fighting off snakes and other demons that were running him into fits. This lasted for hours. Wade said, it appeared that demons were trying to get control in his life. The evil spirits were too much for this man and since his strength was impossible to match, he had to be beaten down.

Wade was not a Christian at this time. Later, he and his good wife did accept Jesus Christ as their Savior. I read to him from various places in the Bible, showing how he was really telling me of Mark 5:1-15, the story of the demon-possessed man.

To complete this event, the following Sunday morning, I played the tape to the group of men, including several pastors and missionaries. Then I passed the knife around for all to look at. We discussed that not all demoniacs were in Africa, nor were they all black in Bible times. There are many around today, but they are not recognized as demon possessed.

My jail and prison ministry has led me to several cases that seem unbearable to the average laymen. A young woman over in Allegan County was possessed of several demons. Sadly, no pastors in this area would even talk of going to see this poor, distressed mother. This 18-year-old would run out into a hard rain, screaming and hollering, tearing her clothes from her body.

One day a strong, Christian, godly woman from Holland went up to see this demon-possessed woman. Yes, she wanted the spirits to leave her so she could be as others of her age. This was determined, so the demons could be removed. The faith of the visitor called, as the Bible requests, "In the name of Jesus Christ, come out of this girl!" These demons were named one by one, and five demons left that young lady that day.

I am aware that very few people believe these stories, but it was the same in the time of Christ. If I gave you the name of this woman, much disbelief would be spread. God's Word is still true even today. I know of several similar cases of demon-possessed people, and all cases were required to be healed in the same manner. Through the name of Jesus Christ and faith, one can be relieved of these demons.

51

How Long, Lord?

When we lose a close loved one, or sadness enters our hearts, we wonder how long should we mourn or continue in the saddened mood. I feel that I learned a very important answer to what we all wonder about, as I sit on the southernmost point of Lake Moultrie in South Carolina. This answer came to me clearly and plainly, of God's plan of a time to sorrow and a time to move on in our lives.

I remembered our own Aunt Susy when she lost her husband. They were truly in love with each other, and Algie's death was a saddening event to all of us. But, Aunt Susy grieved and grieved for months, not changing clothes, never eating regularly or even leaving her home for anything. She would never let anything into her mind to renew or wash away those saddening hours.

I am aware of God's willingness to allow a time of tribute and respect for our dead and for the loss of our loved ones. This happened to Abraham and many of the other patriarchs of the Bible, but how long?

When the family near our cottage on Lake Moultries, South Carolina came out on this particular Saturday, a group of boys came with Steve to fish, boat ride, and enjoy this beautiful body of water. As the boys walked along the shoreline, they found a nest of duck eggs. A large number, sixteen eggs, filled the neatly arranged nest. Steve carefully gathered the eggs up and planned to put them in an incubator to hatch on his arrival in Charleston.

The mother duck watched this very brutal and inconsiderate act. I knew she had been preparing for her family for at least sixteen days. She would not go out flying the normal daily flights with the other eleven ducks. She seemed happy to stay and prepare for her future family.

The following morning, I sat on the bank with fishing poles and bait, fishing for some largemouth bass. The mother mallard came up to me alone, in the saddest mood that could be imagined. She walked with slow and unsteady steps and her quacks were so sad, and in a grieving tone. I knew that she was still in shock about the happenings in her nest. I felt as though I could understand what she was trying to convey to me. I talked to her, trying to comfort and sympathize with this young potential mother duck. It seemed as if she understood. I offered her some of my fish bait, but she would not eat the worms or the minnows. She was close to my side all the day. The other ducks were out flying around on their regular route for food and fun. Later that afternoon, they came sailing back to their landing in our yard, but Sad Sally would not mix in or have anything to do with the other friends. The next morning, when the sun had everything nicely warmed up, and the gang of eleven ducks set sail for other parts of the lake, Sad Sally was missing from the gang. All day they were gone again, but as they did the day before, they returned in the late afternoon to look for their missing buddy.

Now the sadness was the same as the day before. She would not eat, did not want to swim in the water, only to quack in the most sad monologue. I would talk to her as I would pass this poor bereaved duck. I wondered what God's plan was to cope with this distress and sadness in the duck families. How long does this last?

The following day was the third day of mourning. The other ducks left shore at the usual time with no Sad Sally near their side. The flock returned early, approximately noontime. They flew straight to the saddened mother mallard and began to flog her and peck her as she would try and to flee the abuse. It seemed as if all the ducks were determined to get her to go with them.

Sad Sally began to fly; the other ducks blended in around her and all sailed together out into the big lake. Later in the evening, all the birds came home together. Never did I see the beautiful mallard hen in a mourning attitude again. They continued together, to search the banks and water for food. They all gathered in their regular place for the night.

It seemed that the mother mallard had passed through the valley of sorrows and was going on with her life, thanks to the care, concern, and compassion of her friends. Sometimes, it must require stern but loving action from others to bring us out of our saddened slump.

I felt I had just learned another good and valuable lesson from God, as He guided this young mourner on to another part of life. It was as though He said to Sad Sally that three days and three nights are enough. "Continue on in life."

52

GENESIS 28:22 • LEVITICUS 27:30 • MATTHEW 3:8 • LUKE 18:12

Tithe—
I Can't Afford Not To

Since the day that Louise Bates and Red Farabee were married in June 1937, tithing has been a must. My wife was a more concerned and a faithful tither than I was. I just gave things away to anywhere, never too much concerned about an organized system of giving back to the Lord His portion to use as He decided.

Yes, wherever and whenever we received any pay or reward, we saw God got His ten percent soon. We never quibbled about the odd cents, etc. Would God understand that we helped that old woman pay bills or get food, and consider that as a part of our tithe? No, we never considered shortchanging God.

We came to Holland, Michigan in 1954, very undecided about where to cast our lot, or what church to join. We were always faithful to find a church and settle down to work, but slow to do that here. So, Louise put the weekly tithe money on top of a cabinet, in a special bowl, until we became settled within a church.

Dave, our youngest son, became ill soon after our arrival here and he was admitted to the local hospital. His physical problem pointed toward pneumonia, We were very concerned about him because he had a bad case of pneumonia when he was a six-month-old babe. He was a seven-year-old in a strange location, so I stayed close to him for days. But, the most important fact in this story is this: I paid the hospital bill and brought Dave home. Louise asked me how much the hospital bill was and when I told her, she looked up in the big bowl that held our tithe money for the past several weeks. Lo and behold, it was exactly the amount I had paid for our hospital bill.

How could we not be faithful in giving our Lord His portion? Can we steal from God? Yes, I hear people say they can't afford to tithe. Well, we firmly say to all, we cannot afford *not* to tithe.

I could tell of so many occasions when I have not only been convinced of the importance of this, but warned of its significance. I pray you will not be guilty of trying to steal from God. It is intriguing how many times, and with how many methods, God teaches His children important lessons.

53

2 CORINTHIANS 10:12 • LUKE 12:48 • 1 TIMOTHY 6:20

Stand Up
and Be Counted

The income tax man had a habit of trailing me each year. He could not believe that I would pay as much as I had claimed on the tax paper. A steel man ever tithing was unusual, but I love to be called in. I felt that I stood on solid ground. I have noticed, and this I do not understand, meek Christians being used by the ungodly superiors. How do we handle this?

A good friend of mine, a tax preparer and a good Christian man, knew of my upcoming appointment in Grand Rapids, Michigan. He wrote a message and sealed it in an envelope. He asked me to give this to John tomorrow morning. This I did. I wondered what might have been in the note, but John read the note before me and said, "nice."

I told John, "I am a Christian. I believe exactly what the Bible says, to enjoy a full and abundant life. I am not the kind of Christian to get down and lick your shoes, I am a child of the King. I want to be honest in my dealings with all, only wanting what is mine. Now, let us begin our work." I was honest, I was kind, and a good listener to John. We enjoyed the adventure and left as close friends to go to the coffee shop. Yes, Christians must stand up. How could we be standing on more solid ground than

God's Word? I won ninety percent of my request with John. As Christians, we do not stand our ground, we back up, calling ourselves humble. When we have God's Word and His Spirit to support the Word, why should we prove to be so pitifully weak? We should not be ashamed of being a child of the King.

"They measure themselves by themselves, and comparing themselves among themselves are not wise" (2 Corinthians 10:12).

54

ECCLESIASTES 11:1

Rewards

When you check your mailbox, what do you wish to receive in the mail? Do you want to receive a check everyday? Ha, Ha. This is different, but my, how my heart is blessed to receive mail in which a friend, or someone I have been corresponding with, writes to me saying, "Red, I have been saved. My wife and I both belong to Jesus." I must stop everything and give thanks again for this miracle. It is thrilling to have a small part in their conversion. When I am approached at barbershops, down at the mall, or in various places, by someone who comes up to me to acknowledge their faith in Christ—yes, this is worth it all.

I must tell you a very simple case of a happening inside Ottawa County Jail, Grand Haven, Michigan. We were preparing for a Sunday night service in our special room. The inmates were entering and, as usual, I met them all with a personal statement of greeting and welcome. This makes me feel personal as I speak to the group. This particular evening, I looked down the hallway toward the private cells and noticed a young woman who looked about thirty-one or thirty-two years of age—but my, what a mean, tough, even dangerous looking woman coming my way.

I almost had to attack her to get a handshake. This night, the Word flowed freely. I gave my testimony and elaborated on the potential of us all having a full and abundant life. I felt that hearts were stirred. Testimonies were honest and plentiful that evening and I went home rejoicing.

Two months later, I came back to the same location for the same purpose. I was greeting all that chose to come our way, when I looked down the hallway toward the women's cells and I saw this same woman coming my way. She was smiling and, in her hand, she held a Bible and a reference book for a study course sponsored by the Forgotten Men Ministries. I knew that something had happened. She sat at the end of a row of five women, clearly wanting to hear all that was being said.

I prayed about referring to her in my part of the program, but was relieved of doing so. I do not wish to embarrass anyone in our services, but I could not reject this move. I went over to her and told her of her behavior just two months past, and of what a tough demon-looking old gal she was. Now today, she had a beautiful smile, a new expression, and she was studying God's Word with great intent. I asked her what made the difference? She said had been saved a few days ago and life was now meaningful for her and her family. I had to throw my arms around her and praise the Lord for this—another miracle before our eyes. Things such as this keep me going on faithful to His commandments. Again I must say, my beginnings, my background, my personality have all groomed me for this type of ministry.

Thanks be to God, I have stumbled through some tough rebukes from so-called Christians, even called bitter names, and it seems to make me more determined to continue business as usual. If we were all willing to use our talents as God has placed them in our lives, many more would share the great Kingdom of God. I can easily see where my travel, my studies, my experiences, mixed with God's blessings, have made me tough, determined and learned for the battle Satan has laid before us.

55

PSALM 121:1 • ISAIAH 41:6

The Support of the Guide in Turkey

While I was traveling through Turkey, I was compelled to see, again, God's care and protection directly in action. I must say, He sent angels, or directed help, to protect His own.

We were in Istanbul visiting a most treasured place in Europe: Alexander the Great's Museum. There were treasures beyond imagination: a solid gold elephant, approximately twenty-two inches high, given to Alexander by some world ruler; the largest diamond ever cut; and many, many more treasures, guarded by approximately six men. We had been traveling for several days, to various places, with a young lady guide. She was entering her senior year at the University of Ankara, Turkey, and was a brilliant and helpful person.

When we entered this building, we were asked to leave our cameras at a designated location. I had a good camera and checked it in as asked, but I had a small back-up camera in my coat pocket, which I never used. I kept it only in case an emergency arose. While I was standing in a group, listening to the guide describe the value of what we were viewing, my mouth became dry. So, I reached within my coat pocket to retrieve a Cert. My large hand made this impossible without lifting the camera up. A very alert and aggressive guard noticed this and pounced on my back, chattering and hollering as if I was preparing to release a bomb. I dumped him on the floor and walked up to the guide who was in charge of us. I told her to keep the small camera for me, that I was not trying to, or planning to, use it. She nicely told me not to worry about it, and she held the camera as she continued her description of various items. She told the guard, in his language that all would be well and that I meant no harm, but he was not easily pacified and kept grumbling louder and louder. She quieted him down again and he left the room very angry.

As we were leaving this building, my guide was called into a small office to be questioned. I dropped back to the meeting and explained to them the truth of the camera episode. I said I was wrong, that it was all my fault, and I asked that the girl's responsibility not be questioned, or put in jeopardy for me. I said I was truly sorry and would they please forgive me. Well, I received my camera and all was forgiven. We were all better friends because of this intervention for me. Thanks be to God for it could have been very serious for me.

56

The Highway
Raised Up Three Feet

I was in Italy, traveling mostly to places in the Bible that the Apostle Paul had visited during his last years. We left Rome, by bus, on a very beautiful day. Approximately twenty people were on the bus and we all wanted to go to where Paul had landed by ship, at a city named Puteoli. This city is only a few miles north of Pompeii and approximately 200 miles south of Rome. We followed the Appian Way south from Rome. This is a very old road, but well constructed with natural stone. Unusually wide, this is the route they used to bring in Christians from the Far East, by the thousands. Many walked to Rome and the catacombs by this route. Yes, Paul landed with many fellow prisoners there at Puteoli.

When we arrived at the outskirts of the city, we were met by the mayor and his staff. We could see that the highway was raised and the cement broken—it was a dangerous situation. They would not allow anyone to enter the city except for one woman who had a sister in the city, and she was allowed to enter. She was a nurse.

So, we drove on down to Pompeii. This is the city that had been burned by ashes from a volcano a few miles north. The wind blew for fifty-six hours from the North to cover the city with twenty-six feet of red, hot ashes. It happened very suddenly, for powerful Pompeii was a very wicked city, as the signs still reveal. References to sexual practices can be seen in the treasured architecture of brick and stone. Even some paintings of the area show a wicked Roman city. Amazingly, the red hot ashes traveled over a city named Hercules and did not harm it. We drove on South to the beautiful city of Sorrento on the Tyraheheim Sea, where some of the world's most beautiful furniture is made.

I stood on a large cliff at the end of a street in this city of Sorrento. I could see from under me a continuous flow of many white bubbles from pressure under the cliff. Not only there did I see this unusual situation, and when I asked my guide, an older and very knowledgeable person about this, he answered in one word and walked away. This was sulfur being forced from under the area. When we returned late that evening, the city and highway had receded. This was the ingredient used for the destruction of Pompeii.

The Appian Way led by the Coliseum. I was told, as we stood in front of the main entrance, that one acre of land in front of the Coliseum had seen the most blood spilled anywhere on earth. Only those able-bodied enough to run and fight back were used inside the large show and sport place. The others were prepared for the catacombs there on the spot.

The next stop was inside the nearby catacombs. Rome has sixteen catacombs in the city itself, with over 100,000 bodies buried in each catacomb. These have no certain pattern or design inside. While we wound around in the dark, using a flashlight we could detect a small name plate above each body placement. In several places, I counted seven graves one over another.

Now tours to Rome never speak of this part of history. Much of the old Roman Empire structure still stands, for what cause I don't know, but I think our Bible speaks of some important events to come. I was privileged to go down into the mountain prison where Paul spent so many miserable days and nights. It was a large circular area, approximately forty feet in diameter, underground in solid rock. There was a hole in the top, approximately four feet in diameter, with a hook-like rail at one place to lash someone to if they were too sick to be in with the others. Normally, there would have been forty or fifty people at one time. I was thrilled to see a casket in St. Paul's Cathedral, a large church nearby, in which the body of St. Paul is said to be laid. I have never seen such an elaborate artwork laden with gold.

When I see, read about, and meditate on these things, and on how one forerunner suffered and died for the sake of Jesus Christ, I know, more and more, that there is a super helper and enabler who provides the strength and power to invite these sufferings. I long to talk to some of these saints in Glory about things I have seen, heard, and read about.

Meanwhile, we so glibly say, we will serve Jesus if we have time, or if it suits our feelings and schedule.

57

MATTHEW 25:34 • NEHEMIAH 9:5 • PSALM 24:4-5

Move On in God's Plan

I can think of no other person who God has groomed and prepared to visit missions, jails, prison, or any places where we find people "male or female" in trouble, than myself. The Depression years, the years of riding the freight trains—hoboing, the Hobo Jungles, the dangers that lurked within these adventures, the desperate need for food and a place free from cold, damp and wild weather have completed the education I needed to really enjoy this unusual life. Yes, God kept me learning through it all. The war years, the forty years on high steel construction, make me marvel at how and why God protected me through it all. I realize I have made a bold and honest witness for our Lord; I have always been received openly in every place; many have trusted me confidently with things done in their lives; and I have been blessed with a compassion for others in need.

Some of the troubles and hardships, many prayers and personal examples, and the Word of God have left me rejoicing as much as the troubled ones, the sinner reaching out to God. Yes, there are answers to all problems, not in man, but through the power of God in His Word. It would require a book of its own to relate these cases. Drugs, alcohol, dope, thieves, runaways, pregnant girls and troubled boys, bloodsuckers, demon-possessed, abused children and wives—these are sad things to happen in a civilized country. But, sin is the root of all, and only Christ, as revealed in God's Word, is powerful enough to overcome all, regardless of knowledge or ignorance. There is power in God's Word.

I am not writing to gloat about myself, but to relate the importance of being willing to be used in promoting the Kingdom of God with your God-given gifts and talents. As I have said so many times, the people who have their names in God's Book—the Bible—were bold men of God, not cowards.

We must be up and going, to be blessed by the Spirit of God. How can this Spirit move or guide anyone sitting and wanting to keep sitting? We must be willing to be used and "exercise our faith."

I must close this chapter as I began, as I know of no other man that has been blessed as I have in all things. I remarked yesterday, sometimes I feel like Abraham of old.

58

2 CORINTHIANS 11:10

Yes, God Cares for Our Desires

Some of my very first memories were of football. As small kids, we knew every player's name, size, and position at the University of Alabama. Football was in my mind day and night. Even though we had no radios or television in our home, somehow, I learned football. I knew the rules, the good teams, the best coaches, and even good plays and formations to use.

We did not have regular footballs to play with, so we made them from burlap sacks rolled very tightly and sewn with Mom's large mattress needle. We became very good at this process. Mom's mattress needle never made many mattresses for us, but my Lord, the footballs it made.

I dreamed of being a football coach someday. I knew exactly what was required of a good football player. He must be clean inside and out, a hard worker, both physically and mentally, and have a strong desire to be the best. I have used these qualities as a guide in all things of life.

I played college football, but sincecoaches were paid almost nothing, I began to let my life swing away from football altogether. I was just mildly a fan—ha, ha.

When God gave us a large healthy son, I was humbled, but looking at those large hands, I said, maybe he will be a tight end on some good high school football team.

With all our knowledge and wisdom, our Great God is far ahead. He knows our likes and desires, and He can, and does, help us along in enjoying life and witnessing along the way.

We had two sons, born four years apart. This was just right for Mr. and Mrs. Red Farabee. Ben did well in high school, both in the classroom and on the football field. We were made proud and thankful for his achievements—a strong, Christian young man standing firm to his convictions in life.

He was clean of smoking, drinking and drugs—a hard worker in all he undertook. The result of this was a scholarship to the University of Michigan. The coaches came to our home and we talked openly of habits and convictions, and how important they were to real men. They felt blessed to have these two young men, Roger Burrsema and Ben Farabee, enroll at U of M and play football there.

Every night, I thanked God as He kept guiding the boys, Ben and Dave, both on and off the field, protecting and guiding them. I never forgot the many days, when I was a kid, that we would sit under a streetlight in a gravel road crossing and map out new football plays, and what it would take to have a good winning football team. Well, God's plans far surpassed me in all this.

Every Friday night during football season, it was a must to go and watch Dave play high school football. Then, early the next morning, all of us would leave for the big stadium at Ann Arbor. We had regular seats on row fourteen for many years. We all saw Ben play in the Rose Bowl game in 1965. Yes, we were thrilled sitting there. As the game started, the announcer said, "Now let's see what Bump Elliot's good clean boys can do." Well, Michigan won the game, fifty-two to six against Oregon State. Nine of the Michigan boys went to the pros. Ben refused a chance to go to Dallas, saying, "Football has been good for me, but I'm getting out while I'm still in good physical condition."

Dave, our number two son, played great football, both in high school and at the University of Michigan. He received a broken wrist while playing against the University of California and this incident kept me from seeing both of my sons play in the Rose Bowl, four years apart.

This year, 1998, there is a brick in the area of the football stadium in Ann Arbor that is stamped with the words: "Red Farabee's sons, Ben-1965 and Dave-1972 played football here."

I want to express to you that when our lives are turned over to our Lord and Savior, our desires are magnified far beyond what we could ever expect. We never have to turn away from things of value. With God's help and guidance, life becomes far more abundant. I have enjoyed many good years of football, thanks be to our Lord and Savior.

59

2 KINGS 2:2

Faithful,
Yes, Faithful

On one of our trips home from the New Orleans area, a
great lesson was taught to me about the faithfulness of
God and His operation of the universe.

When we entered our home in Holland, Michigan, a strong
smell of fuel oil dominated the house. Since we had been away
for the winter, we had many thoughts of what could be wrong.

We have our fuel oil tank in the basement to supply the furnace that heats our home. I saw dripping from our tank, and
after mopping up approximately three gallons of oil, I saw
where the oil was coming from. I saw a regular drip at the
extreme bottom of the fuel tank, and I began to think of a fast
remedy. How could I get the tank out, and how would I transfer
the oil in the tank to a new one. What would be the best, and
least expensive, answer?

I called the furnace man who had installed my tank and furnace. I told him of my big problem and said that if I could wait
until 4:30 tomorrow, he would have something that may be of
help to me. I was at his office at precisely 4:30 the following day.

He gave me a small item about the size of a pocket watch. I
questioned its ability to do this important job, but I returned

home and carefully read the directions before following them. I cleaned off the surface over the leak and placed the provided gasket over the proper place. I set this gadget directly central over the hole and the tank grabbed it with much power. Yes, this magnetic block was going to do the job, keeping oil inside the tank at all times.

For years the faithfulness of God, His magnetic power, never quivered or faltered. I would lay awake many nights when I was far away from Holland, marveling at how it could be that one small shudder could fill my basement with a stinking, troublesome job to do. But the device never failed for several years. Sometimes I think, "What if I failed to breathe sometime at night, even while sleeping, or maybe my heart might forget to beat a few times?" But no, God does a perfect job of taking care of His. He never fails. Great is His faithfulness.

60

ECCLESIASTES 5:13

Damascus, Syria

After leaving Iraq, we flew directly over to Damascus, Syria. This is one of the oldest cities in existence today, and I don't see many changes made, Ha, Ha.

We were treated well while we were there, and I will not forget the courtesy of one man regarding my camera. I had so many good exposures, within my camera, of pictures taken in Nineveh that I wanted to save. This man helped me greatly and would not take any money.

As we viewed the battleground between Damascus and Israel, I could feel the bitterness and fighting, even though I saw nothing.

I was so blessed by this trip to Damascus. It is hard to get in that area, but I walked down the old street, called Strait, that the Apostle Paul was guided down while he was still blind. It was a narrow street with approximately three elevations at the end where we saw an old building. Down in the lower elevation was a small open room, and at an altar was a sign stating that this was where the scales fell from the Apostle Paul's eyes and he began to see again. His entire world had been different since he had been struck blind, approximately twenty miles outside the city. I was thrilled to see and believe this, and God kept a hand on our shoulder as we traveled to the places the Bible is so clear about. Thanks be to God for this.

While in Damascus, I talked with a young man about venturing over into Israel to do harm. I told him that those Jews would make his head look like a sack of nuts. He laughed and said he had to go, he was drawn to go. Yes, I believe that. There is a special drawing power that is really unknown and unexplainable, but is built on hatred and will not go away.

Here in Damascus the Apostle Paul escaped for his life, as he was let down from a window to leave before he was killed by some of his own. He was classified a traitor, because he was saved for Christ's sake. He fled into the desert for approximately three years, to be thoroughly prepared by God for his special ministry to the Gentiles. I would think that next to Jesus Christ, he was the greatest for God's service.

In Amman, the hotel where we stayed was new and a very desirable place. I sat with the new manager (or owner) a good while. I had noticed that he had a Gideon Bible in each room and I asked him why. He was skeptical when he made the decision to do so, but I encouraged him, saying he would not only be rewarded, but he would be blessed mightily. I gave him a brief testimony of how God had kept, provided for, and guided me through the years. We had a great visit together.

61

PSALM 4:25

God's Care and
a Vision of Glory

On our return trip from a winter in Charleston, South Carolina, we decided to go by way of Memphis, Tennessee where our daughter and husband lived. They had a home in the Waukazoo area. When we left our son-in-law, Wayne, in Memphis, I asked if I could do anything for him in Holland, Michigan.

This was the year I had my 70th birthday, but I was not intelligent enough to recognize it. Wayne asked me to get an estimate from a tree remover in Zeeland and call him with the price to cut and remove five trees in his yard. He had the trees marked with a string around them. I did as I was asked to do, but the suggested price was too much to satisfy Wayne. So, my grandson and I decided to use my chainsaw and some rigging and cables I had, to do this job ourselves. It went well and we had all the trees down in a short time.

I noticed that in a much larger tree, if a certain large branch was removed, our daughter and family could look across the Pine Creek Bay and see her brother Dave's house. They could even wave to each other. I had plenty of time to do this simple task before prayer meeting that evening.

I tied the ladders together, leaned them onto the back of the tree from the limb side and climbed up with the chainsaw to remove the large branch. I was approximately twenty-four feet off the ground and I reached around the tree and sawed off the limb. But it pulled the ladder out from under me as it fell. I knew then that I was in for serious trouble and it came. I threw the chainsaw over into the yard away from the trouble spot, but I fell down across the aluminum ladders and made horseshoes of them.

I knew I was hurt. Matthew told me to lay still and not move while he ran for help. I did as I was asked, but during this short span of time, I felt myself to be on an elevator like the old construction elevator we used so many times when erecting buildings and towers. This elevator went down several feet and stopped. I stepped off and viewed a most beautiful scene: lush grass, rolling hills, and a large, beautiful building on top of a hill.

During the past few years, my family doctor and I had been very close friends. He was a strong Believer, and we could talk freely about our Lord and things of the Bible, but he had an accident in his airplane, north of our area, and was killed suddenly.

As I looked across this beautiful area, I saw Dr. Eli Coats come running to me as I stood a few feet in front of this open elevator. He appeared to be about eighteen years old, full of youth and vigor.

He said to me, laughing and clapping his hands, that he knew I was coming. He just knew it. I said for him not to be too cocky, he only beat me there by 12 days. Not knowing then of the exact time, this definitely proved to be true when I later checked it out on the calendar. Eli went running up toward the big building where I could see people beginning to gather. I turned and entered the elevator, returning to the tree and the ladder with three broken ribs on the left side, plus a fracture on the lower part of the pelvis.

As the Apostle Paul did, I felt I got a glimpse of the glory of heaven. I had often wondered about our age in heaven and all I saw were very vibrant and youthful people just running about as birds fly. This was very interesting, yes even to me.

The ambulance came and checked me out and prepared me for the stretcher which would carry me fifty yards up a steep area of lawn. I suggested that I walk, and I did with great pain and one stop along the way. I was in the hospital for five days and returned home as black as could be from the shoulders to the knees. I questioned the ability of God to remove all the black from within, but He did in about three more weeks.

I didn't want to miss making a garden that year, and began to check the condition of the Roto-tiller, etc. Within a few days, I had the Roto-tiller on my small trailer going to the small engine repair man to make it able to start.

When I was bringing it back home, the mechanic helped me to load it up, but on arrival home, I wondered what would be the best and easiest way to unload it. After checking with my neighbors for potential help, I learned all four had bad backs. I sure didn't want to injure their backs any worse, so I walked up to the machine, picked it up and put it on the ground. This sounds strange, but my God in heaven knows I have never had any trouble with my back since. Thanks be to God for a great lesson of trust, plus a beautiful view of glory. Thirteen years later, I thank my faithful Lord for His daily care for me. I learn more, each day, of His desire to keep me active for His Glory.

62

PROVERBS 27:24

Iraq

All of our careful planning, praying and waiting finally began to pay off. We had a strong desire to visit the impossible places our Bible spoke of so much. The Garden of Eden; the Land of Ur; Old Babylon; Nineveh, where Jonah dreaded to go; Noah's hometown of Fara; these names were as a dream to visit.

There was one flight by an Iraqi airline scheduled to leave Cairo, Egypt at three o'clock in the morning on Sunday, and our desire was to be on it. We received a telephone call from Chicago while we were preparing to leave our hotel in Cairo for the flight to Baghdad. The call apologetically reminded us that we were not to go into Iraq with any literature that had the word Israel on it. Well, this covered most of my books, maps, etc.

I saw a young man who looked American to me, coming down the stairs in the hotel. I told him of my situation and, again, he was an angel from our Lord. He was an employee of Johnson Controls in Minnesota and he was coming directly to the U.S.A. He brought my censored literature back for me, thanks be to God. As planned, I called him on my return and all was safe.

The flight to Baghdad was beautiful. A full moon seemed to cover at least a third of the sky, a perfect reminder of Sinbad and others, ha, ha. We were taken to the second best hotel in Baghdad and we were received and treated well, even though we had three men who constantly stayed in our presence. Remember, we were a group of archaeologists from Chicago, Illinois. We would select where we wanted to go, what to see, and get to ask questions. Our number one man was Albert, a guide and strong government leader, a great, likable man of approximately fifty years of age. We were to stay in our hotel every morning until he arrived. Then, he and the other men who were always near, a Trans-World representative to protect us, plus an interpreter.

One thing that has impressed me very much was that we were in the country of Iraq, where the Garden of Eden lies, where the Tigris and Euphrates rivers run together. But in the Izraf Museum, the statue of the first man and first woman stood side by side, and the winding serpent was between them. We can read this in our Bible, yet we could discuss this freely with these men.

We rode our old wreck of a train all night, down to the Land of Ur on the Euphrates River. It was very hot and people by the thousands were moaning and hollering all night every time the train would stop. I was glad to see the sunrise then. The old walls and ruins there were still detectable, as was the size of the house and location, for the pitch is still rising from the ground at one location. I climbed to the top of Tower of Babel and looked over the old city remains. This was the only place in Izraf where my camera was removed from me. There may be a question in some people's minds of this being the Tower of Babel. I saw nothing any place else to lead me to believe otherwise. No, not even in Babylon. I was in London four years ago at the British Museum, and now they have confirmed that the same place in Ur was, and is, the remains of the Tower of Babel. Approximately forty feet high now, you enter the top four ways on steps. Then there is nowhere to go but up. It is flat on top, but God intervened. Some believe they planned to go to heaven, but I believe that there were so many different kinds of gods being worshipped in that area of Babylon, and in all the plains surrounding, that they planned to be above the other gods in height only. A study of Babylon and their gods show there were a great many.

I was thrilled to climb around in where the old furnace area was in Babylon when Daniel and his friends were cast in the furnace. Only the general location and the burnt, black soil led us to believe this. On the south side of the old city of Babylon was Belchazzar's palace and the handwriting on the wall. I found a part of a cup there and brought it home. I treasure it today.

I walked down to the river, but the course was different during Daniel's time when he said, tonight is the night of Belchazzar. I was talking to a local worker there, and he told me that the large statue of the Lion of Babylon had been in the swamp area nearby and had just been lifted out and put on new footings on the bank of the Euphrates River. This Lion had been buried there from when Babylon was destroyed over 2,500 years ago. Except for certain areas, Babylon now lies under about twenty feet of sand. We detected where the one-time famous Hanging Gardens hung from a third floor structure.

Nineveh is only twenty percent uncovered today, but much can be seen underground at various places. Nineveh is buried under eighty or ninety feet of soil, but some very beautiful gates still remain in places. The city is across the river from Monstad, the largest city in Northern Iraq. I was talking to Albert, on our last day, about a future trip there to visit his country. He told me that when we left Iraq, there would be one other group coming from Germany. After that group, there would be no more. Within a few weeks after we had left, Iran and Iraq began shelling and bombing each other and thousands died during the lingering war. It almost seems as though it was all organized just to thin out those thousands of people. Who knows?

63

ACTS 9:36

Wait for the Coon to Move Out

A few weeks ago, our Pastor, Mike, preached a sermon about some differences between women and men. I don't always absorb all of every sermon I hear, but I remembered this section well because, as so many times before, this point was brought very vividly before my eyes.

We live in a small section of trees and woodland and we love it here. So many times, we see deer, wild turkeys, or other semi-wild animals. On this evening, I was sitting and reading when in came our very good and caring neighbor lady. She does a good and consistent job of checking in on our every need.

As we were sitting in our living room, I heard an occasional "urk." I was not too concerned about what, or where, it was, but our neighbor heard the "urk" and looked straight toward me. I never responded in any fashion. Again the "urk" was repeated. She could not contain herself any longer and asked me if I had heard that noise? Everyone knows I don't hear *all* the noises, ha, ha. I replied, "yes, I heard that," and she seemed to feel somewhat relieved. Again it returned, "urk, urk".

She asked, somewhat under control where I thought it was coming from? I told her, I thought it was coming from my chimney. Karen jumped up and asked, "What is it?"

I told her, "maybe a coon." This was as if a bomb was preparing to explode. She said it would tear up chairs, couches, and wreck everything. I continued unconcerned and she sat down and asked me if she should go get Gord, her husband, and have him bring his gun over. I said, "No, I don't think that is necessary." Her next concern was what was I going to do about it. I told her I would maybe crack the fireplace vent and burn a newspaper in the firebox to let them know they were not welcome there, and hopefully they would move out. Well I did, and a coon came out onto our housetop smoked and groggy. We stood in the yard, and Karen kept saying, "shoot him, shoot him." I was still reminded of Pastor Mike's sermon, that women were far more emotional than men.

I told Karen that if I shot that large coon and killed it, I would have to go to my pole barn and retrieve a long ladder to mount the roof and get a dead coon. Then, I would have to bury him the next day. Also, if I just injured the coon, it would go back down into the chimney with the small ones and would die there. I said again, that I believed if we would just leave all alone, mother coon would move her family from that location tonight.

Well, that is what we did, and the next morning early, a call came from Karen wanting to hear of the end to the coon story. I reported that it had a happy ending and that all was well here at home. The coon and family had a brand new home somewhere. I did say that I believe when God made this world, He made it large enough for me and that coon, ha, ha.

This story has much to teach us. First, don't react at your first thought, without considering the good and the evils. So many times when we react on the first impulse, it can cause many problems later. I say, wait on the Lord, ha, ha. Thank you Pastor for another lesson from God's Word.

64

JOHN 10

My Name Is Called

We, as people, sometimes get foggy-minded trying to understand all that we read and believe in our Holy Bible. I learned a new scriptural fact at the Memorial Parade yesterday. Please read carefully. My wife and I arrived at a good place to see and cheer the band participants. We unfolded our chairs and prepared to enjoy a good parade. Sitting near me was a young family sitting very comfortably together—a mother, a father, a small child, and a beautiful, big, brown dog.

This dog was so comfortable and relaxed that I asked him if he was ready for the bands to pass. He seemed to answer my question with a yes—ha, ha. I could feel there was a great interest for the whole family. Many good bands passed, car horns were blowing, and people were hollering to each other. This was a great parade. It seemed this dog could not care less. He was just a great, quiet, withdrawn spectator. I could not fail to recognize his reverence throughout the whole parade.

The large, school-children's bands, with the smaller kids and their horns, created much noise as they marched by. The cheering crowds continued and the beautiful dog, who had been so perfectly behaved, leaped up and yelped, standing on his hind feet and facing the band.

I was so amazed, I asked the mother if the dog knew anyone in the band? The mother said, yes, the dog's young friend was in the band and had called to him by name. I never even detected the voice from the passing band, but the dog heard and recognized the voice and his name. His response was thrilling to us all.

As Jesus Christ stated many times in the scripture, He knows His sheep and they also know Him. This was so clearly brought to me in a shadow of the real truth. This dog heard, and sure let it be known. I left the parade thrilled, not so much by the action and sound of the bands, but by the clearer understanding of God's Word on this subject. Yes, my prayer and understanding of our Good Shepherd will be more personal. I truly believe He knows my name and He can, and will, recognize it.

Please read John 10 in a receptive manner.

65

PROVERBS 22:6 • ISAIAH 60:22 • ECCLESIASTES 4:13
LUKE 2:40 • MATTHEW 18:14 • MATTHEW 18:10

No Time for Children

During the past few years it seems as if all we can read about or hear on TV is to gather up all the guns when a sudden event happens. I have never understood the motive of this. It sounds so immature. Surely, any sane person can know what makes a gun explode fulfilling its design to do just that.

Any sane parent or adult would not leave guns on tables to attract children or normal meddlers. Surely, the liberal people now in leadership seem to love to play with guns or drop bombs from afar. Many innocent women and children are killed by this cowardly act. This has been going on for months and nothing is gained except more graves. The pictures I see on TV, and in papers, show that the ones getting kicked and killed don't have the guns. The man with the gun survives. Why not give guns to the men and adults being assaulted, burned out of their homes, and killed? Supply them with guns and ammunition to protect themselves, instead of being do-gooders and killers.

The memorial service following the terrible Columbine massacre showed some of the school children praying, our leaders praying, and a whole nation supposedly praying. Why could they not be allowed to pray in the school building? There was much talk about God, but why could a Bible not be found in the public schools? This is very hypocritical indeed.

Now, the gun-grabbers disclose that the answer is to gather the guns, and that the parents are bad for not being able to detect that their child is not being loved enough and is thinking bad thoughts. Our greatest psychologists can't pick out the bad kids from the good ones. What a joke on our great advisors.

I asked our son, Dave, if he was interested in seeing some of the memorial service of Columbine High School. He said, "No, I have seen enough." He had been to four funerals in one month of West Ottawa students all killed by cars, not guns. How could we improve this situation? Would you choose to remove the cars from certain people?

My good young neighbor was shot to death in their home a few years past, and no one has been found guilty of this horrible crime. These things happen in our area also. I read in the newspaper of old people being broken in on and beaten to death by some misfit after drug money. The true fact we face today is that I don't want anyone to even think that Red Farabee doesn't have a gun in his house. This thought could lead to some bad things.

Why not be honest, the survivors have guns both at home and in wars. Our founding fathers still knew of the evil dangers ahead when it was written that we should be allowed to bear arms.

If all the guns and ammunition were retrieved, we would be as other pitiful people we see in our countries, with nothing to help our resistance from evil forces. Yes, it could happen here, even under our present leadership. This is a serious problem for America and we must face it fairly and honestly. We have a generation of kids that have never been taught and disciplined. This sets the stage for serious things to happen. Even small children could and would kill their mothers. Dad, as parents we must choose to live with them, daily holding the children's hands and teaching them in honest Christian love and companionship that will last through their lives.

As I was told, at a young age, by my Dad—"that shotgun is dangerous, don't touch it." I believed my Dad and I would not touch that gun at any price. Now, these forever muddlers prowl through every drawer and pull out all things. Yes, a gun there would be of great interest to him.

What is the answer? I talked to a policeman about this this morning. This problem leads to the parents' hands and attention, their love, care and compassion. Or do they prefer to leave the children to someone else and so they can more money? The decision of the parents shows up early in the child's life. God has a plan for us all and if we rebel and choose our own way to cope, of course we lose the battle.

66

PROVERBS 28:20 • MATTHEW 6:19

The Modern Day Methuselah

One of the mot inspiring events happened to me a few years
ago in the suburb of Summerville, South Carolina. As I
was spending some prime time sitting, writing and listening to
the Charleston news station, the news came out that this day
was the birthday of the oldest man known on earth, Mr. Willie
Dewberry of Summerville. I knew it was only a few miles over
to Willie's home, so I rapidly prepared to go see him and sing
Happy Birthday to him on his 119th birthday.

I thought there would be a big assembly of people and news-
men by the time of my arrival, but there was no one there. A small
three-room house in the midst of many is where I found the oldest man on earth, lying on a worn-out couch in a dark room.

There I began to feast on many treasures which seemed to
have been prepared by God for this day. I went to the home next
door to Willie's and introduced myself to the woman who lived
there. I told her I was visiting Willie, and asked her not to let the
Michigan car tag excite the neighborhood. My intention was
good and I longed for a visit there. This move cleared the air
with many people. I did sing Happy Birthday loudly and clearly
even to the neighborhood.

Willie was easy to talk with and his sharp mind was astounding to me. His eyesight was good, much better than mine and his ears were working effectively. The thrilling faith he was eager to talk of was like that of Enoch.

Questions about the Civil War were no problem for him to answer as his dad was in the middle of this terrible event. Willie remarked that his dad had told him, "Willie, I pray you will never have to do what I have done today. I have walked all day on dead bodies, sliding in their blood." He had never forgotten that statement. He told how the country was raided for its prime timber, which was then shipped out from Charleston to the North. The cotton fields were gleaned and loaded for places in the Northeast. Some of the most interesting and educational subjects, I was able to were discuss with a firsthand student— "one on one."

I visited with this dear man many times. I would even take my wife with me to ask him questions and listen to his great wisdom. My grandson, Mike—an airline pilot—visited with me and offered a ride on a plane. This, Willie quickly refused as too unsafe and dangerous. I asked him one day to let me see some of his battle scars from his many fights and battles. He said to me, "Red, I have never had a fight in my life."

I looked out at his neighborhood and remarked, "How did you keep from having fights? You must have been a fast runner." He answered, No, when he was a small boy, his mother told him that if he thought in any manner there was going to be trouble somewhere, just don't be there. He had always tried to do that and, at 119 years of age, he had received no scars from others.

Willie loved his Lord. "Why not?" he said. "He has provided for me the necessities of life. He keeps me safe from harm." Willie had no enemies to his knowledge and he was not bound to the evils of the world—no TV, no telephone. He owned a radio at one time, but he said the evils of it overrode the good, so he gave it to someone else.

As I sat on the couch with Willie, I could feel as if I was being clothed by our Lord and Savior in all things, a great and secure feeling of knowing that here is a child of the King. The material things were few. Maybe the old worn-out couch, a bare table, and a chair or two were about all his major earthly belongings, but his blessings were many: his long life span and a clear mind filled with fond memories, and his continuous love and faithfulness to our Lord Jesus. His family was limited, but I had to label Willie Dewberry a Methuselah of this century.

Willie was called home two years later. Many never realized there was a special person in their neighborhood—one guarded and blessed by our Great Shepherd. How foolish we are to scramble for material things in this life and fail to reap the things of true value.

67

JOHN 3:7

The Early Worm

I have never had such an important lesson revealed to me as was the year of 1998. Please read carefully about this truth.

This was a very bad year for my apple crop. I have almost seventy fruit trees here near our home and most are apple. I have apples of all varieties. I try hard to be an honest apple grower and not to abuse the habitat for the others involved. I know this same policy is used by most parents. First, I realize the important value of our honeybees in pollinating the crops and vegetables. I realize their population is decreasing each year, so to be a good apple grower with much compassion for the pollinator, I refuse to spray the apple trees when the apple blossoms are present. Just before the apple is formed, approximately two weeks later, I spray strongly and faithfully and I see beautiful fruit form and grow. I spray a special spray to remove even the small attempt of a scab from approaching my beautiful apples.

When September arrived, I gathered a gallon of the best apples to deliver to my wife for making pies. On my next trip through my wife's kitchen, she repored to me that only two apples were without worms or signs of worms. I was so shocked to hear this.

181

The following week, I read an article about a report from a convention of scientists. Yes, this is true, the worm was set before the apple came and the beautiful apples were born with a worm within.

This is also true of our beautiful babies: so innocent, pure, clean and sweet smelling—beautiful. But, as we read the Bible, we find the serpent was there first. I have noticed in our children as babies such demanding screams, such cries, as if they were being murdered for little or no reason. Then you begin to wonder if there is rebellion at this young age. As the months pass, these actions occur quite frequently. Yes, we try to cope with this problem, we "spray the apple again," and think all is taken care of. Later years bring much spraying and treatment to the children's behavior. We even evaluate them by their appearance, hoping and praying that our specimen is perfect. But, at the most desired test or period of scrutiny, we find a faulty product. The worm has never left its habitat.

The only remedy for this behavior is through a conversion to our Lord Jesus Christ. He is the only method to change a sinner into a saint (Romans 3:10,22,23). Then, when we are ushered into the kitchens of God, there will be the good fruit of service to Him. Again, God's Word proved itself to me.

68

PSALM 33:12 • PROVERBS 14:34

Our Country's Condition

A few months ago, I was in Judge Roy Moore's office talking with him. The decaying situation of these United States was, in general, the topic. Judge Moore is a strong Christian judge that some have tried to crucify for having the Ten Commandments of the Bible hanging in his courtroom. This Alabama judge carved those words in boards when he was a young man and he believes them enough to put all his future on the line for this purpose. He has gathered much lay support, although some high court in the United States is displeased with his stand.

I encouraged Roy never to back up one inch on his belief. He is standing on a solid rock and should hang in there true. He really has more support than it appears on the surface. He impressed me with his plea for Christians to have the courage Joshua spoke of. If not, we are going into slavery, and fast.

The pulpits are too silent about God, country, patriotism and family. The present generation knows very little of what this country has endured, so that we can sit idly, or lazily by. Patriotism is a joke anymore. Sin has passed by us, and we know nothing of its being and its effect. This has not just happened, it has been designed this way and is working beautifully for the liberal believer. I say, liberal beliefs are like trying to push a rope up a hill. There is no sound basis to think from.

As we hear much from the younger generation about the cruelty of the manufacture and use of the atomic bomb, I have followed this cause from the first. And the last is not here yet, please watch carefully. A scientist from Chicago had the formula for the bomb and knew of its potential power and destructive ability. He was hesitant about making the decision and he thought it over for many days while watching the progress of the war. He also saw the wickedness of the people. Germany fought brutally. Japan forced this war by the bombing of Pearl Harbor on a beautiful Sunday morning. If there had been no Pearl Harbor, there would be no atomic bomb. This saved many American lives, maybe their country.

I worked on the atomic bomb job in Oak Ridge, Tennessee and know much of the situation that the United States was forced into. Yes, some numbskull would even go around wearing, and boasting of owning, a belt made of "Jew skins." This is truly sick and wicked. God requires punishment for such acts. Japanese soldiers captured Americans, cut their tongues out, and ran them into caves on the island. Then gas was spewed on them and they were burned alive by the hundred. These were American boys, and these sick and spineless traitors of Americans, stand up and protest the atomic bomb with such brilliant and flowery words. It is sickening.

Our Bible says capital punishment is supposed to be for three causes: for being a traitor, for rape, and for murder. Look what we cater to today and hold so giddy. How can we be blessed of God? War is Hell, but people are desperately wicked. We try to paint over these truths as if they are not there.

May we be open and concerned about how our forefathers prayed, fought, and died for this country to be a livable place. Please cling to their truth in prayers, faith and integrity.

69

1 CORINTHIANS 15:57

Get Over on
the Other Road

I was speaking at the local City Mission and as I closed I asked, as I always did, that anyone who had a serious problem troubling them would come by and see me. We would talk the problem out using the Word of God. On this particular night, I had six troubled souls to console and strengthen in God's Word.

A very neat and well-dressed man came to me and wanted to know what the Bible says about his situation. I was truly saddened to hear his history and the past of his life. He had married here in Ottawa County many years ago and his marriage crumbled soon thereafter. He left for California, found work there, and dropped out of circulation for thirty-seven years. He had never married again. His wife had filed for divorce, but it was never finalized. She is still living here now, having never married again or had anyone else in her life, and he told me the same of himself. This man was sixty-four years old, was back in the area and doing very well financially. God had blessed them both during the last thirty-seven years, but he asked me about getting married and what would be the right thing to do.

I told him how I sorrowed for their past and I suggested he go to see her the next day and say, "Come on now, we have so much of our lives to make up or refill." I told him to leave behind stubbornness and rebelliousness and to travel on with God at the helm of your lives. I remarked that thirty-seven years was missing from the middle of their lives.

Another case was a young man who came to me in the sorrow of having gotten a girl pregnant, who had then left for Texas. She wanted to get married, but he didn't feel ready for it. After a short, honest, godly talk, he was telling me that he loved her and that she was a good girl, much better than he was. So, he vowed that the next day marriage plans would begin to be developed. We prayed and praised God. He left a happy young man.

This night I also took a boy back to Hamilton, who had run away a few days before. His stepfather had asked him to leave as he did not want to abide by the rules of the home. We discussed them and laughed, honestly talking the complete situation over. I told him, with my hand on his shoulder, that if he wanted to make an old man happy, he should return home, crawl into his bed and say, "I am home, Dad." We solved this very important problem that night—happy dad and a happy son. God can handle all our problems as well as things we just think are problems. These problems happen only when we begin to move away from God's Word. Keep that Bible under your pillow.

Many, many troubled people have come to me in the missions, in tears and sincerity. I know no other solid and true answer except what is found in the Holy Book.

One night as I shared, I spoke strongly to the alcoholic and the drug user. I told them that if they did not change their course in life and give our Lord the reins of their life, I knew what their future is. I know there was a dumpster just outside the door, half full of dirty trash. I looked them in the eye and said that their future is out in the dumpster. The choice is theirs.

A few months later, I read in the paper how some great liberal thought this City Mission should change their policy and remove the preaching and teaching of the Bible. The newspaper had interviewed some of the people in the mission. I will never forget the picture and this man's statement on the policy. He said, he came there a worthless person with no future and no hope, but one night an old man told him if he didn't change his life and reach for his only hope, which was Jesus Christ, his future was in the dumpster to be dumped into Hell. He told the press that he believed that old man. Now he is working a good job and saving money, a happy man. God forbid removing God's Word.

70

HEBREWS 2:3

Escape

This is what I had in mind, and only that, when I ran through a cornfield to catch a freight train in Moscow, Tennessee. I found more trouble as I tried to grab the train for Memphis. The special agents and police were waiting and set for me. So, I crossed through the train and into a bank building, trying to escape. The persistent officers kept coming, so I ran down through the small town. They kept running after the kid who had merely committed trespassing on railroad property. I saw they were determined, so my escape continued. I ran through town, jumped into the Wolf River, and swam back under the bank to hide in some tree roots. Some hours later, they gave up their search. I had eluded them for a season. I am trying to illustrate the price we sometimes pay when we try to escape something, or someone.

I worked many days in Atlanta, Georgia, building and erecting fire escapes, a much needed item after the Winecraft Hotel fire there, when 119 young girls dove to their death from the ninth, tenth, and eleventh floors of that hotel. Some jumped from windows across the street shredding awnings and leaving parts of bodies hanging on braces. The water and blood ran for three days down the gullies into sewers. Sad, but there was no way of escape.

We tried to perfect this many times as I gathered with groups of hobos to hear the conversations. I could gather that a large percentage of these people were running, looking for a place to escape to. The wrongs of their life led to this—looking for a day by day escape.

I see what some in jails and prisons plan and do to try to escape. Much planning is done and much hard work, but it never works out as planned.

Sin is anything done or said contrary to God's will. A sin of commission involves things we have done that we should not have done. We commit sins against our brothers and God. These things we try to flee from, or deny, or rub them off as not so bad, but we are to be judged by the Word of God. We have these rules at our fingertips, at all times, but we try to escape clean.

Sins of omission are those things we have left out or failed to do. Yes, God remembers those failures we run by. Sometimes we even fail to say "thank you." This can be a troubling sin. I remember well, when I graduated from high school, a certain man gave me a white shirt for a graduation gift. As time went on and on, I did not remember thanking Lon Cleveland for the white shirt. This was my only white shirt and this negligence of mine troubled me much. So years later, I drove many miles out of my normal route at night to thank him. He was a security guard for Goodyear Fire and Rubber Co. and I felt greatly relieved from this added weight when I finally did what I knew was right. Failure to do what we know to do, is wrong. A few years later, I heard Mr. Cleveland had been called home. So many times we try to escape our duties as a Christian to satisfy our own wills.

The missions are filled with people running away, or trying to escape something or someone. So many young boys and girls leave home to escape some minor dislike, only to find far more problems in trying to escape.

Many tunnels have been dug by people trying to escape, then at the other end they find this has failed. Many have spent sleepless nights in cold conditions, hungry and dirty, trying to escape from something, then finding the problems are multiplied.

As an older, matured man, please let me introduce you to a sure way of escape. There is no other way to go or hide:

- Job 1:15
- Psalm 124:7
- Proverbs 19:5
- Matthew 23:33
- Hebrews 2:3

If you will do as I did as a sixteen-year-old boy, underneath a freight train in Montgomery, Alabama, you can rejoice that you have found the way of escape that leads directly toward Glory. You will feel your Guide and Helper's hand on your shoulder at all times, to supply the power to continue on without failure. Repent and Believe.

- Ephesians 2:8-9
- Romans 10:11
- Romans 6:23
- Luke 19:10

71

PSALM 16:8 • EPHESIANS 6:14

Stand!
And Be Prepared
to Cope

This lesson is another that requires total action, as if your life is depending on it. We have been asked to put on the full armor of God and stand against the enemies. Yes, we say that we believe this teaching and also do it, but sometimes we feel the armor that God gives us is not sufficient, and our first and rapid decision is to flee.

Please think on this illustration and its results. My neighbor friend was telling me of how another little "David" stood firm. This man lives on the outskirts of the city and these streets and corners were a perfect place for the people of the city to drop off cats, dogs, and whatever else. The people of the city had become tired and did not have the compassion for these pets they once had. The bad winter days were used by many to drop off the animals and run.

I have always been taught that dogs cannot survive out in the wild elements, especially in Michigan. But, cats have a strong, tough heritage and have a much better chance of survival under similar conditions.

This problem proved to be big trouble for this rural family. The challenge was so great that he provided for himself two bad dogs. These were trained to be killers of all these strays. The dogs loved their work and made a big success of killing cats and dogs that had been discarded. One was a vicious pit bull, and the other was a much meaner animal.

Again, a few stray cats were thrown out of a moving vehicle. The dogs saw this and ran to the scene. The usual response was to run, so away the cats started running. Needless to say, they were soon caught and their bodies riddled by those vicious dogs. When the dogs returned to their house, it was a surprise for them to see a small cat—a nice, clean, well-mannered pet, approximately half grown—standing in the dogs' yard.

When the dogs ran to the cat, it would bristle up as if to say, Come on. She was prepared. Several attempts toward the cat were made, but the results were the same. The dogs would back off. Not willingly did they leave the cat alone, but they feared the uncertain results.

This is similar for a true believer of Jesus Christ equipped with God's Word, plus a strong, never-faltering faith. There are so many positions on which we should stand firm for our Savior, but we immediately choose and execute a retreat. God does not approve and bless this kind of so-called Christian, for our testimony and power is shattered.

Yes, we are now living in Satan's world. We see it on all fronts. But, as God's Word has so clearly presented, we can be victorious with His help. Please, I beg of you, don't run when opportunities arise to stand for our Savior, Jesus Christ. You will be a winner if you stand firm.

72

MARK 4:28 • JOB 10:22 • 1 CORINTHIANS 2:7

Right Way
or Wrong Way—
Bean Vines

There are so many unanswered questions in God's plan, it stumps our intellect. The most brilliant people never devise a sensible answer. It is easy to prove all beans are left-handed. When they are young and begin to grow up a pole or object to cling to, it is always, left handed or grows toward the left.

I have tried to think why this is so. I think of sunrises and air currents, but I arrive at no sensible answer. I have a grandson that pilots planes for United Airlines, and I have asked him on Project #1 to look into this when he is in South America, thinking maybe south of the equator there would be some right-handed beans. God's plan and facts of nature are always true and for a purpose.

When people have tried to change this growth pattern by winding the vines the opposite way, they will always die. The report is that they die of a broken heart, because they cannot have their own way. I say that they would rather die than go in the wrong direction.

Then, also for an unknown reason, hops—a vine that produces blossoms and pods used for making beer—always winds to the right as it grows. Why? God's plan continues to work perfectly. In the same way, a person's life is productive when operating within God's will.

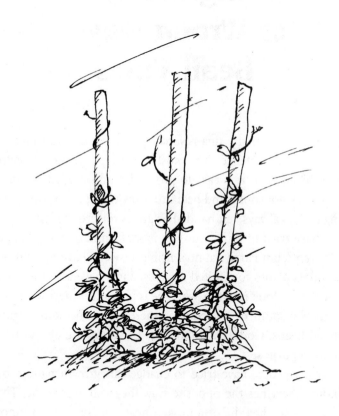

73

EPHESIANS 5:25 • COLOSSIANS 3:16

Where Are the Christians?

During my entire life I have suffered the most severe blows of critical words from supposedly Christian "fellow believers." I am saying, beware of the wolves in sheep's clothing. They may be sitting near you. I hope you receive these words as danger warning signals.

During the early '60s it seemed as if Satan took complete control of America, a country built on strong Christian leadership and holding the Holy Bible as a guide. God guided this country into a strong godly system in schools, legal systems, churches, homes, work places. The U.S.A. was the leading nation of the world. America was honored by God and all people of the earth.

Then, Satan engineered the movement following the Second World War. A sad mistake was made by the parents, soldiers, and people of that era. The following statement was made so much: I don't want my children or grandchildren to have to go through what I have endured. Think of how Satan used this. Punishment and harsh methods of discipline were forbidden to the following generation, thanks to Dr. Spock and friends. It was noticed at once that the generation of baby boomers was high in numbers. This was to be a bad thing, as they were a rebellious generation, protected by the legal system and experts in the education field. No right or wrong was taught, no punishment was pursued. The college was to lead, and the leading professors were formerly rebellious professional students, given these positions as leaders of the next generation.

I say this to let you know where I stand on this movement. I say that the so-called Civil Rights Laws can, and are, being misused and misunderstood by our sick politicians and the cheap lawyers of today. Now the psychologists are coming into the picture scrounging for dollars. I say neither are around unless there are some great possibilities for financial gain.

I was teaching a class of adults in a Bible class. I was teaching on the minor prophets and Israel's return from 70 years in Babylon. When I teach, I teach hard, honest facts and use scripture at all points. I let my many years of Christian experience work together lessons of truth and godly challenges for the future. Yes, this class of baby boomers knew I was raised in an Alabama city and this paved the thought that I was a racist. This is totally false, but I was never asked to teach again.

When I was a small child in a family of a mother, father and six children during the Depression days, we were taught right and wrong, godly doctrine, and a great respect for all others. My best friends were black people. I played with black and white alike. My dad and mother would discipline me terrible if I even used a smart word against anyone, even black mothers and kids. Later, after periods of time when I would be away, my black friends were always faithful to visit me, and we would fellowship together on my return.

I have fought white boys over snobby remarks about my relationship with black people. I have never felt otherwise, but phony thoughts about my being a racist have been fabricated against me because I am from the state of Alabama.

During my hobo days, I was held up at knifepoint, throat scarred, and robbed of all my clothes and shoes. I was then left bleeding from a cut under my left arm. Would you believe these five black men in Chattanooga, Tennessee were the same men I had just given a loaf of bread, sandwich spread, and a package of bologna to eat. Yes, I heard some great thank you's then, but one hour later everything reversed.

I am saying this, that I have no envy or hate of anyone for this sad event. First of all, I am a Christian and I don't even think of such things as revenge and hatred. My heart has been greatly blessed by so many Christian people. I shall never forget them.

Many times when I was working in the South, I would pass on to black Christian men on our jobs, Christian literature for them to use in their churches at no charge. We would sit and discuss Bible truths for hours at a time. Our relationship was great together. Thanks be to God for the many lessons I have learned from these dear people. Yes, it does upset me to hear these remarks from someone so glibly. But so many of these remarks, we must shrug off as ignorance.

When I had retired from steel work, I went to Louisiana and purchased four acres of land in a suitable location that we would enjoy. There was plenty of good fishing nearby and alligators were plentiful in that area. There were many bad snakes in my backyard, Ha, Ha. The nearby swamps were filled with life as God has made and left it. This proved very intriguing to a retired high steel worker, so we built a house there.

There was a good, black friend who lived nearby. He was retired from a large paper mill and his family was off living their own lives, except for his wife. Frielder Burton was a good Christian man and known as such by all that knew him. We fellowshipped together regularly and he would bring vegetables he had raised, to my wife. One day, he asked me if I would show a slide presentation from Israel at his church, which happened to be black. Sure, I did this for many of the churches in that area—black or white—it never made any difference with me. My presentation would never change. Jesus Christ was the total answer, and the Bible was God's direction for us *all* to march and to live by. My heart was humbled so many times by the singing and rejoicing of these dear souls.

When I was home, I would do small building jobs for different people. I would never charge my wages—not a cent, but I would ask Frielder to help me and always gave him the pay. It was always good to be in his presence.

We had just completed a small garage attachment for a person on this particular evening, when my good friend went to be with his Lord. The minute I was told of this, I went to Mrs. Burton and offered my condolences and sadness to her. I said if there was any way I could be of help, to please let me know—such as a problem with an insurance policy, legal matters about her home, unpaid bills, etc. Above all, she trusted me to be a big help.

That evening Mrs. Burton called me to ask if I would guard her house until she returned from selecting the casket at the funeral home. She lived in a black neighborhood, and doubted the safety of her things until the children gathered in to help her get things together. A friend and I sat in a truck with guns to protect the drive to her house, as she had requested. All went well until she arrived home at approximately 10:00 p.m.

The next morning, she asked me to have a part of Frielder's funeral. This I accepted with great humility, for I knew his past well and she asked me to speak for at least twenty minutes. I spoke, and felt honored to be asked to do this.

Then why was I so used of Satan to be called a racist within my own church? We must stand strong against sin whenever we find it. I tell these events for the total purpose of returning to the Bible. Not as you want to, but as God presented it to you.

If God tarries, and this generation of children with their own children can live, it will be as animals. Many will die young.

The knowledge of God will be severely limited. "Who will carry the Word?" We have schools that deny God, politicians who laugh at God's Word, parents who know little about spiritual things to cling to when it is needed desperately, and no time to think.

I find it very hard to find anyone with a good, strong knowledge of God's Word and promises to have fellowship with. They are either too busy or they don't know. When I speak of our Lord's return to get His bride, the ideas are thrown out, and sometimes even laughed at, by so-called Christians. Sad, but true. Where do I go from here?

I pray our churches cling to God's true Word and not lean into social issues to be popular within our culture of 2000. Remember we are to be judged by God's Word.

74

HEBREWS 6:15 • 2 TIMOTHY 2:3 • HEBREWS 3:6

Curing and Enduring

During the war years of the early '40s, I was inspired to go present my abilities and knowledge for the total purpose of protecting the U.S.A. and my family. Construction was a must. All kinds of new plants were needed and that required manufacturing and installing of new and modern machinery. This is where I entered into installation of all types and kinds of precision machinery. I selected and purchased the best and most precious tools possible to buy, as I wanted to do the very best job possible.

There were very few precision levels that were graduated down to .001 of an inch, but I was fortunate enough to get one of these—one of the first on the market. I treasured it with the finest of care and protection, and it traveled across many states by my side.

When I left Redstone Arsenal in Alabama, there was a terrible need for this precision level at that plant. I made the decision to donate it to the war efforts there in Huntsville, Alabama. I thought I could somehow get another one for myself. This proved to be foolish thinking.

I learned from the manufacturers that this was impossible because of the time and curing process required for the metal to make this particular level. I was informed that this special metal required seven years of laying outside in all kinds of weather to cure. From sub-zero temperatures in the cold Ohio winters, to the 100 degree hot sunshine, plus the electrical storms that frequently passed through the Ohio Valley. After seven seasons of this type of treatment, the shaping up for a finished precision level began. Only this type of care and treatment made material suitable for this best and most precious product.

After much time and trouble, I found another of these valuable tools. But, during those long months of waiting, I would think of a favorite Bible character—"Ole Job." Every day I would think Ole Job is curing for a special Job. I would hear the young, eager and even aggressive employees at the plant say, "Let us stop the curing process and use them now."

But, the great Chieftain would say, "No, not yet, son. The time is not right."

This has been a great lesson to me in many ways since then. I received my precious level in due time. As an old man, now cured and strong, looking over the past at the important events to make this so, I realize many of my best lessons were learned during the testing months of the Great Depression of the '30s. The hard struggle for life, all the time preparing for the better days ahead. The food we ate was what we could find and get. The green food, the wild fruit, berries, combined with the beans, etc., from a garden. This proved to develop the fine boys in a most perfect condition. We longed for other foods, but this is what God provided for us.

Our best lessons come from "times of curing" and "patience and enduring." We must go through the valley to get to the hilltop of Glory.

75

The Thorns
and the Roses

The days of riding the freight trains from place to place during all kinds of conditions were very vital in preparing me more and more. The long days when meals were sometimes postponed until another day, gave me much time to meditate and search into life for positive things. Patience was a must to endure. Yes, I traveled as I could, as the railroad schedule provided. The food came as people, yes other people, were willing to give.

The beds were not made of great mattress material. Sometimes, I spent nights just bumping on top of a boxcar lashed to metal parts of the trains. Maybe a cardboard box in an open place would be my bed, maybe the floor inside a building, covered with lice and bugs. Sometimes I spent the night running from special agents and police shouting to kill, even for being on the railroad property, and sometimes I was beaten off the train with sticks and clubs.

I mention the bad and sad things to help you relate to the process of curing for me. I think I used those days in the proper fashion. I was humbled. I had to be. I was strong. I had to be. I was made grateful for everything. I learned to respect and understand them. I had to. I learned to care and feel for others, for I realized how small and useless I was within myself. My whole life depended on others. With God's help, guidance, and the assembling of so many of these parts together, I am today a totally caring and tenderhearted, understanding person.

I feel and say so many times at missions, jails or churches, etc., that I will never live long enough to repay people for all that they have done for me. As the Apostle Paul said, I am indebted to the cause of helping people.

Now, I can see all along the ways of life where I have been cured by enduring and learning into being a different tool for the cause of Jesus Christ and the Kingdom of God. Otherwise, I would not have been strong or tough enough to carry on in this mixed-up, out-of-order world of today. I pray you will understand, this is not of myself, but my heavenly Father selected me for Himself from under a freight train in Montgomery, Alabama in 1932. I totally accepted then. I had to. I can now see and feel the way that all things fit together along the way in life. My purpose is to be found faithful to my Lord and Savior. I know of no other person who has been blessed and rewarded as I have through it all.

I thank you for reading this. I pray as you travel through your valleys in this life, don't be angry, don't be discouraged, be strong, be encouraged. God is hammering you into a more useful vessel to be used for Him. Yes, we must be cured for strength and endurance to be of real value. (Read Job 31:23-25.)

76

Ivol—Love

Here are a few words that I want you to think about. If we could paint a life, what would we paint? Would we say as the steel maker would "shout"—put more charcoal in the pot to make it stout.

We need more ore to make the metal more strong.
Add the limestone until the impurities are gone.
Turn up the heat until the pig iron melts.
Look inside the furnace where the ingredients are kept.

This is a product not often to be found
all bonded together, very solid and sound—
a shining example of the best to be made,
not of material that will tarnish and fade.

The precious metal edges get dull in time
and need rubbing and polishing to be made to shine.
We may need to sit back to ponder and rest.
As the diamond cutter looks and prepares for the best.

When curing and testing in life take their place,
the true qualities arise and come to the outer face.
So, Ivol, when we see your beautiful smile,
we see the real ingredients that you cannot hide.

The *faith* you have shown to many you meet
has transformed lives forever to keep.
Where do you get the patience and enduring power
to keep looking up and never become sour?

The curing and training to us brings a new twist,
brings out many good qualities, not room to list.
When thinking of bad things, we must endure.
All this is required to make the product more pure.

I have watched you gel into a treasured stone—
made of great qualities and a value not known.
Even your name when turned, twisted and cured
spells "LOVE" a name that is precious and pure.

So when we think of a life to draw,
I don't think of a product in its raw.
But the Master produces a precious stone
from an ole rock many passed left unknown.

(This lesson was written and read to our daughter as she
was suffering her last months from the terrible disease of can-
cer.)

77

LUKE 11:4 • GALATIANS 6:1 • MATTHEW 18:21-22

Forgiveness—Yes

Please read this lesson carefully. I think this is the most important lesson for anyone to really learn. So many say, yes, yes; but prove not so. Read.

One of my best friends was lying in the local hospital in critical condition. He was a man of ninety-one years of age and he had never told me of any close family ties. He had never discussed this in several years. I was so concerned about Bob that night, that I walked into a small room and talked to three nurses. I asked them what they looked for when life was leaving a human being. These nurses were friends to me and they responded with three points: 1. The color behind the ears, 2. The color of the fingernail area, and 3. The color around the feet and ankles. I said I had noticed that Bob had two of these and possible three. The nurses agreed.

I thought seriously of plans for the next move. I learned of Bob's daughter in Tampa, who never had any type of fellowship with her dad. I wrote to Mary, introducing myself only as a good friend to Bob, and told her of his physical condition at the present. I felt as if it was my duty to notify her regardless of whether there was a close relationship or not.

On Saturday morning, Mary called me. I told her how everyone loved Bob and that he was a good one. She bounced back to tell me what a wicked old man he was and how mean he had been. I listened to this poison flow, hearing how badly her mother had been treated and how she had to marry soon and leave home to keep from being killed.

I asked if she had any children and she told me she has a son—a missionary doctor in Central America. I asked if she thought he cared, or would come to Michigan to see his granddad. She replied, "Lord, no, he hates that old man."

I felt we should approach the problem as God's Word says, so I asked her if she was a Christian. She said, "yes, sure," and mentioned a very large church where she attended. They had just hired a new young man from Michigan, a fine preacher.

I told her as humbly as I could, that I could not understand how anyone could cry out to Jesus Christ for forgiveness and then not forgive their dad or others. At the very least, Bob is a human being and God loves him. I said the venom that should have never been, has been spewed for three generations, poisoning lives, ruining families, shortening lives. I said that Jesus Christ came to eliminate this. How could she do this? Whether she loved her dad or not, he was a helpless dying person.

She asked me if I would do something for her and I said, sure, anything within reason. She said, "Red, will you buy a box of chocolates and give them to Dad?" She told me she would send me a check for them. I told her that I was going to do this anyway for Easter, and forget about the check. I also asked, "What do you want me to tell him?"

She said, "Will you tell him that I love him?" I had to cry knowing that the Holy Spirit was at work on the phone to Tampa. I promised to keep her informed of his health condition.

I did this the next day as promised. Mary had sent him a box of his favorite candy. I kindly questioned Bob about past times and about how tough it was during the Depression days. Yes,

Bob says it was a trying time to live in. I agreed and asked him if he had any family problems that were so deep from wounds that had never healed. I will never forget what he said next. He looked me straight in my eyes and clearly said, "Red, I am just as clean as God in heaven can make a man. I have no envy or hate against anyone. My heart is filled with only love." And he repeated, as I had asked Mary, "How could I ask Jesus Christ to forgive me when I still hold envy and hatred within my heart?" I was so moved I had to change the subject. I told him, "Mary says she loves you and have a great birthday also." She was mailing him a letter and card.

Since this event, Bob has rallied in his health. His daughter came up to see her dad and spent a day here, even though she had to leave her husband at home with Alzheimer problems.

This blessed my heart. Three generations foolishly divided came together through the power of God. Are we traveling on this old, dirty, ungodly route through life? If so, it is not necessary.

Almost Home

As you read this book, I pray that you will see and understand that life is a journey. That journey begins in a sinful, wicked world filled with temptations to beset us and to influence us away from a living God who gave us life, with a soul to check back to Him when our last breath leaves us.

As the directions that have been left for us to travel by, the Bible leads to a full and abundant life for all who really believe it. The only way to gain these rewards is through Jesus Christ our Lord—the only One who can open the door for us to enter far better things when this life leaves us.

When we fully surrender all things in this life to Jesus as our Lord, we will see and understand more, how our great Creator and Guide desires our fellowship with Him. Yes, we will also yearn to draw closer and closer to Him—the One that died for us so that this may be possible. This happened when we were running from him.

As the songwriter has said, in such a beautiful form, "Each step I take just leads me closer home." The Bible is very simple and clear on the fact that obedience is followed by blessings far more than ever expected. Please recognize them and give Him the praise and glory.

Disobedience is followed by bad things. They may be called cursings to Israel, His chosen people. I thank God daily that I made the all important decision of my life at an early age, and that I have had a constant feeling of His hand on my shoulder to guide me and help me all along the way of life. This true assurance of His constant presence has made it possible for me to be used by Him, whenever and wherever I am. My life has been a great adventure.

A few weeks ago, I was talking to a good friend of things to come according to God's Word. As we discussed the troubled conditions in this world and yearned to see or hear some answer to cure the world's problems, we only found hope in our Lord's return to gather in His own. But, as we have been warned in His Word—keep on, keep on winning other souls for His kingdom until He returns. There is a great reward for the faithful few.

As Randy and I had our arms on each others' shoulders, we spoke of our expectations of heaven. Randy asked me, as a much older person, be sure and look his dad up if I get to heaven first. He remarked, with tears in his eyes, "I know he is there and maybe my uncle is there. Please find them and tell them that I am on my way." I replied that I would and we shook hands as a symbol of a solid promise.

Please don't wait too long to prepare for the exit. When your soul is checked back in, I pray it was used wisely for Him.

—G.L. "Red" Farabee

A Hobo's Journey Toward Glory
Order Form

Postal orders: Red Farabee
14995 Ransom Street
Holland, MI 49424

Telephone orders: (616) 399-1056

Please send *A HOBO'S JOURNEY TOWARE GLORY* **to:**

Name: _____

Address: _____

City: _____ State: _____

Zip: _____

Telephone: (_____) _____

Book Price: $12.95

Shipping: $3.00 for the first book and $1.00 for each additional book
to cover shipping and handling within US, Canada, and
Mexico. International orders add $6.00 for the first book
and $2.00 for each additional book

Or order from:
Books, Etc.
PO Box 4888
Seattle, WA 98104

(800) 917-BOOK

or contact your local bookstore